Are you su

Behind them, with a loud metallic thump, something large landed in one of the funnels. There were two more thumps in other funnels, and James's eyes widened with anticipation. He walked over to look inside the funnel and saw a very large, and very strange, spider.

"Extraordinary!" he said. "Miguel, look at these markings!"

Jerry gulped. The size of the spider was horrifying.

"Don't just stand there — take pictures," James said.

Jerry kept his distance. "Are you sure it's dead?"

"Yes," James said, already moving to another funnel. "Quite dead."

Carefully, Jerry approached the funnel, his camera ready. He was focusing, about to shoot, when the spider suddenly convulsed, then reared up. Startled, Jerry kicked the cone over, then instinctively stamped on the spider, crushing it.

High above them, in the tree, the other spider — a much bigger spider — shook with silent, shrieking spider fury.

ARACHNOPHOBIA

ARACHNOPHOBIA

A novel by Nicholas Edwards
Based on the Motion Picture from
HOLLYWOOD PICTURES and AMBLIN ENTERTAINMENT, INC.
Executive Producers STEVEN SPIELBERG and FRANK MARSHALL
Based on the Screenplay by DON JAKOBY and STEPHEN METCALFE
and WESLEY STRICK and
Story by DON JAKOBY & AL WILLIAMS
Produced by KATHLEEN KENNEDY and RICHARD VANE
Directed by FRANK MARSHALL

SCHOLASTIC INC.
New York Toronto London Auckland Sydney

ISBN 0-590-44228-7

12 11 10 9 8 7 6 5 4 3 2 1   0 1 2 3 4 5/9

Printed in the U.S.A.   01

First Scholastic printing, August 1990

ARACHNOPHOBIA

Chapter 1

The rain forest was strange and beautiful and mysterious. The vegetation was thick and green — and full of danger. This was a land too wild and primitive for mere human beings to survive. Somehow, the forest's beauty made it seem all the more threatening and alien.

And yet, deep in this Venezuelan jungle, there *were* human beings. Americans. Scientists, to be precise. They were gathered at a small base camp, loading up a helicopter for the day's exploration.

Below the base camp, a narrow wooden boat made its way slowly up the Orinoco River, deep in the heart of the jungle, surrounded on both sides by dense foliage. As one Indian guide steered the boat, his passenger, Jerry Manley, looked out uneasily at the jungle. Jerry was a freelance photographer, so he went wherever an editor sent him on assignment, but going off to the jungle wouldn't have been his first choice. It wouldn't have been his *tenth* choice.

The native guides maneuvered the boat past

three thundering waterfalls and up to a muddy riverbank. One of the Indians hopped out, pulling the boat to shore. Jerry climbed out less gracefully. He looked around at the bustling base camp, as men worked to load crates of equipment into a helicopter.

Seeing the man who had hired him for this job — James Atherton, a professor of entomology at California Polytechnic Institute — Jerry walked over to him, his sneakers sticking in the mud.

"Dr. Atherton, I presume?" Jerry said, cheerfully. "Hey! Hey, wait up. Not so fast."

"We're in a hurry, Mr. Manley," James said, not breaking stride. "Just leave your personal things here and bring your equipment. We're going right up." James was in his late thirties. He was tall and aggressive — a man who loved adventure. His specialty was the study of insects, and he was very ambitious. He was a man who sometimes took too many chances.

"Sorry I'm late," Jerry said, trying to keep up. "I've been laid up in Caracas for a while with a fever. If you want to know the truth, I'm not over it yet."

James ignored that, indicating another man to his right, who was also dressed in jungle boots and khakis. "This is Miguel Higueras," he said. "Miguel, Jerry Manley."

The two men shook hands. Jerry felt a little self-conscious about the fact that he was dressed in civilian clothes while the other two were outfitted for the jungle. Jerry was wearing jeans and sneakers — both very muddy — a Hawaiian shirt, a photographer's canvas vest, and a Miami Dolphins cap.

He had a camera bag draped over one shoulder and two cameras slung over the other. It was very hot. He took a small towel out of his bag and wiped the perspiration from his face.

"Be sick on your own time, Mr. Manley," James said. "I want closeups of all the specimens, and coverage of the surrounding *tepuis*."

"The what?" Jerry asked blankly.

"*Tepui*," James said. "It's Indian for 'mountain,' where species have survived in isolation for millions of years."

Jerry grinned, checking his bag to make sure he had enough film. "Any man-eating dinosaurs?"

Miguel grinned, too. "Only Atherton here," he said. "Fewer than half of the *tepuis* have been explored. You're in luck — we're hitting a brand-new one today."

To Jerry, this didn't sound all that lucky. "Anyone ever get lost?" he asked, careful to sound casual.

"Legend says that men who climb to the 'rain desert' never return," James said, then winked at him. "Don't worry, we 'small-game hunters' don't climb, we fly."

Up ahead, a helicopter was being warmed up, its rotor blades noisy in the early morning quiet. Three Indians were already sitting inside the chopper. One of their foreheads was marked with a distinctively shaped tattoo.

"Who are they?" Jerry asked.

"They're our guides," James said, with vague disinterest. "Stick close, and they'll show us the way down."

Jerry nodded, gave the two Indians a thumbs-up sign, and climbed aboard. James and Miguel were right behind him.

Slowly the helicopter lifted off the ground, climbing into the sky and and leaving the security of the base camp far below. They flew high above a thick blanket of white clouds, catching occasional glimpses of the savage jungle below — hot, green rain forest, rushing rivers, deep gorges.

Jerry looked out through the open 'copter door and put out one arm to steady himself, not noticing the huge black ant near his hand.

"Veinticuatro!" said the Indian with the tattoo.

Jerry looked over at him with some confusion. James leaned over and calmly knocked the ant off the doorway and out of the helicopter. Reacting well after the fact, Jerry yanked his hand away.

"Twenty-four-hour ant," James said.

"They bite?" Jerry asked.

James nodded. "They can kill you, Mr. Manley — in sufficient numbers."

"So can some of the frogs here," Miguel added. "Don't touch any."

Jerry looked from one to the other, not sure if they were putting him on. "Great," he said finally, and stuck his hand inside the safety of his vest pocket.

The helicopter flew on, almost seeming to float above the clouds.

" 'Why shouldn't something so new and wonderful lie in such a country?' " James asked. " 'And why shouldn't we be the men to find it out?' " He paused.

"Arthur Conan Doyle — 1912," he said, identifying the quotation.

"You seem to have a severe case of 'tepui fever,' " Jerry said.

James, not amused, leaned forward to study the map Miguel was holding. "This is where we're going," he said, pointing to a spot on the map.

Jerry leaned forward to look at it, too. The map was a satellite survey of the tepui. One odd-looking section had been circled in red marker.

"We'll land here," James said, pointing at the circle, "and then walk. It's a sinkhole. Years of streaming water wears the rock away."

The helicopter was close to that part of the jungle now, flying above overgrown ledges along the immense rock wall. From cracks and holes in the wall, water gushed out as though, somewhere behind the rock, a huge water pipe had burst.

Jerry leaned out of the 'copter bay door, snapping pictures. Next to him, James gazed down into the bottomless pit of the tepui sinkhole.

"At least two thousand feet deep," he remarked. "It's very dark at the bottom. You'll need flash equipment."

The chopper began a slow descent towards a rock clearing. Jerry had to swallow — the length of the drop was making him very nervous.

James looked down at the dark rocks below, feeling a thrill of excitement. *He* could hardly wait to start exploring.

Chapter 2

The helicopter landed in the small clearing on the top of the *tepui*, and the men climbed out and started to unload their gear. They would carry as much high-tech scientific equipment as they could manage in their metal-framed backpacks.

They made their way painfully over a rocky landscape, their boots — and Jerry's sneakers — clinging to the wet ground. Gradually they worked their way down the edge of the rock crater.

James pointed out a fan-shaped plant. "*Stegolepis*," he said. "Edible, and nutritious enough to survive on for weeks."

Jerry wiped his brow with his sleeve, perspiring heavily. "I'll pass," he said, and looked around. "Look, let's forget about the fact that no one mentioned poison ants, poison frogs. But a two-thousand-foot drop? Come on!"

"Don't worry," James said. "Our guide will show us the quick way."

Jerry shrugged, somewhat grumpily. "So, plants," he said. "They your specialty?"

"Insects and spiders," James said. "And identifying new ones."

"Just what the world needs," Jerry said, and wiped his face again. "More bugs."

James wasn't offended at all. "What's *your* specialty, Manley?" he asked.

"Football," Jerry said.

Ahead of them, the Indian guide had stopped in his tracks, refusing to move.

"¿*Qué pasa?*" James asked, passing him.

The Indian answered in rapid Spanish, and James sighed, then shrugged, and continued on his way.

"What's with him?" Jerry asked.

"This is as far as he'll go," James said.

Jerry stopped, too. "What?"

"Just come on," James said impatiently.

All around them was the sound of dripping water, as moisture gathered on leaves and moss. The lower they climbed, the darker it got.

James was carrying a small device that registered temperature and humidity levels, and he looked down as it beeped.

"Amazing," he said. "Air temp just went down another ten degrees in the last two hundred meters. We're almost there."

It was very, very quiet. It was very, very dark.

Jerry took picture after picture. The camera flash lighted up the area around him with brief flickers of illumination. Absorbed in his task, Jerry accidentally stepped backwards into a large spiderweb. He was trying to untangle himself when something fell down in front of his face. It was a dead parrot, caught in the same sticky, silvery silk.

Hearing him yell, Miguel stopped walking and looked back. "Jerry, you all right?" he called.

"What was that?" Jerry yelled. "Get it off me! What is it?"

Miguel came back down the trail and helped untangle him from the web. "Just a parrot," he said. "Be careful, you're too big for us to carry out."

"Thanks for your concern," Jerry said, a little embarrassed that he had reacted so strongly.

Miguel laughed and went after James, who was well ahead of them.

Jerry shivered slightly and pulled strands of web from his clothes. Peering through the nearby branches, he saw the rest of the web. It was larger and more complex than he would have imagined. An eerie shaft of sunlight made the dewy strands look almost like gold thread.

Jerry shivered again, snapped a couple of pictures, and hurried down the trail.

High above him, Jerry was being watched. But he wasn't being watched by two eyes, he was being watched by eight — a spider's eight eyes.

The spider watched the men invading its part of the forest, and it darted along a tree limb to follow their progress, swift on its eight, angular legs. It was very swift — and very angry.

In the meager light, James and Miguel had finished setting up equipment beneath the canopy of a towering tree. Jerry sat down on a nearby log, feeling tired and sick from his fever.

"What's that stuff do, anyway?" Jerry asked, too ill to care much about the answer.

"Ever throw a large firecracker into a pond?" James asked.

Jerry shrugged. "Maybe, when I was a kid. Why?"

"What happened?" James asked, in the overly patient voice of a teacher.

Jerry sighed, rubbing his face with his sleeve. "All sorts of things floated to the surface," he said.

James nodded. "Exactly. Everybody ready?" Without waiting for an answer, he turned on the machine. Instantly, the air was filled with smoke, as the insecticide rose into the air. James waited briefly, then turned off the machine.

"Prepare yourselves," he said.

"For what?" Jerry asked uneasily.

"Pictures, Mr. Manley!" James said. "Take pictures!"

All around them, insects started to fall. Jerry ducked as they bounced off his baseball cap and cameras, doing his best to snap pictures.

James and Miguel had set up funnels all around the clearing, and the funnels were slowly filling up with insects. Gradually, the insect "rain" stopped, and James and Miguel began to collect specimens.

"What's that?" Jerry asked.

James held up a beautiful blue iridescent butterfly. "I think it's a new species," he said. "We'll call it — *Photius Manlii.*"

Behind them, with a loud metallic thump, something large landed in one of the funnels. There were two more thumps in other funnels, and James's eyes widened with anticipation. He walked over to look inside the funnel and saw a very large, and very strange, spider.

"Extraordinary!" he said. "Miguel, look at these markings!"

Jerry gulped. The size of the spider was horrifying.

"Don't just stand there — take pictures," James said.

Jerry kept his distance. "Are you sure it's dead?"

"Yes," James said, already moving to another funnel. "Quite dead."

Carefully, Jerry approached the funnel, his camera ready. He was focusing, about to shoot, when the spider suddenly convulsed, then reared up. Startled, Jerry kicked the cone over, then instinctively stamped on the spider, crushing it.

High above them, in the tree, the other spider — a much bigger spider — shook with silent, shrieking spider fury.

James was also pretty angry, as he grabbed Jerry's arm and yanked him away from what was left of the spider.

"What do you think you're doing?" he demanded. "I *need* that spider."

"It was alive," Jerry said, still shaking.

"Don't be ridiculous," James said.

"Professor!" Miguel called, staring at the specimen jar where he had placed one of the other spiders. "Look! *No está muerto.*"

"That's not possible," James said, stunned. "They should be dead." He took the jar and stared at it in disbelief. The spider banged against the glass, going for his hand. "Very aggressive," he said, frowning. He turned to Miguel. "We'll take two back alive and preserve two."

Miguel nodded, taking out a bottle of alcohol and some cotton swabs so they could suffocate two of the spiders. He handed a soaked swab to James, who dropped it into the jar in his hand.

"Are you sure that's going to do it?" Jerry asked.

James nodded. "This stuff would kill an elephant."

Jerry watched as the spider slowly died. Then he sank down onto the log where he had been resting before. Watching the spider suffocate made him feel very, very ill.

The huge spider up in the tree was also watching the spider in the jar die. It didn't like to see other members of its species killed. It scurried up and down the tree branch, aiming a murderous, hissing shriek down at the men, poison sacs on each side of its body vibrating rapidly. The shriek was terrifying. Suddenly, the spider scurried down the side of the tree trunk — a nightmare on eight legs.

The shriek was a warning that the men couldn't understand.

Chapter 3

James decided that they had collected enough specimens, so they began packing their equipment to
leave. As Miguel hoisted his pack onto his back, the
spider raced the rest of the way down the tree
trunk, leaped into the air, and landed on top of the
metal frame. It clung there briefly, then disappeared inside the pack. It was very angry — and
it was going to go along for the ride.

The climb up the rocks was much worse than the
climb down had been. As the men concentrated on
keeping their footing on the slippery rocks, they
failed to notice the body of a dead tapir lying behind
a log, its head partially cocooned. Another very
large spider was wrapping it up to eat later.

"I've never *seen* spiders like this," Jerry said,
out of breath. "What do you think they eat if they're
this big?"

The other two men were too out of breath to
answer.

Once they were back at the base camp, James

went right to work in his outdoor lab, beginning a careful dissection of one of the dead spiders.

Jerry stood nearby, looking out at the beauty of the *tepuis* in the distance. He was very tired and, if anything, his fever was worse.

"Incredible," James said aloud, as he worked with a tiny scalpel.

Jerry wandered over. "What is?" he asked.

James looked up. "The spiders. They have no reproductive organs. Almost like worker bees or soldier ants."

Jerry looked at the huge spider carcass without much enthusiasm. "If these are the soldiers, I'd hate to see the generals," he said.

James laughed and kept dissecting. "How are you feeling, anyway?" he asked.

"Terrible," Jerry said. "This fever's killing me."

"You don't look so good," James agreed. "Get some rest."

Jerry nodded, turning to leave. Behind him, Miguel upended a huge bag, and a shower of dead insects spilled out onto a sheet. Jerry shook his head in disgust and walked away more swiftly.

The two Indian guides had placed the loaded pack frames near Jerry's tent. Jerry walked past them and into the tent. He sat down on a cot, then slowly put a light meter and some film canisters into his camera bag.

Outside, the spider appeared, one leg after another, as it climbed out of the pack.

Inside, Jerry took a bottle of pills from his pocket and swallowed one, taking a gulp from his canteen.

Then he shivered. He took off his shoes and stretched out on the cot, and pulled up a blanket. He shivered again, then closed his eyes.

Outside, the spider scuttled through the grass, towards the opening of the tent. It waited until Jerry was asleep, then climbed up onto the cot and disappeared underneath the rumpled blanket.

Jerry tossed and turned restlessly in his sleep. Aware, suddenly, that something was different, he opened his eyes. He stared at the bulge racing up his leg underneath the blanket.

He tried to kick it off. He lifted the blanket and saw red eyes and glistening fangs. As he tried to knock the spider away, its fangs sank into his hand, drawing blood.

Horrified, Jerry recoiled from the bite, too stunned to think for a minute. He tried to scream, but then, the neurotoxins in the spider's poison slammed into his brain like a freight train. His jaw locked as he started to go into convulsions. He gripped the cot with both hands, his eyes bulging with sheer terror.

The spider retreated slightly, watching Jerry convulse. It crouched down, waiting to see if enough poison had gotten into Jerry's system.

Jerry tried to crawl off the bed to get help, but his body wouldn't work. The neurotoxins had done their job.

Miguel, who was coming into the tent to get something, saw him and ran to get help.

"¿Señor? Professor! Come quick!" he yelled.

James, who was about to dissect the second spider, dropped his instruments and ran over. Miguel motioned towards the tent, and James followed him inside.

"*Esta muertó*," Miguel said. "The fever."

James bent over the cot to see if he could help.

James looked at Miguel, shocked. "I can't believe it," he said. "He's dead!"

Unnoticed, the spider crawled down to the tent floor and retreated to a dark corner. It was pleased. Its poison had worked well.

Chapter 4

After Jerry's unexpected death, the Indian guides, with Miguel's help, assembled a makeshift coffin and gently placed Jerry's body inside, in preparation for its return to the States.

James, dressed for travel, stared off at the distant *tepuis*. "Did you collect his film for me?" he said. "Have we notified his family?"

Miguel nodded. "I contacted the American consulate."

"Okay." James sighed. "We'd better seal him up."

As they turned to get the rough wooden cover, the spider came scurrying out from the underbrush and climbed up and into the coffin. By the time the men had carried the cover over to the coffin, the spider was out of sight.

James and Miguel placed the cover carefully on top of the coffin, and the two Indians nailed it shut. Once again, the spider was going to go along for the ride.

* * *

At the airport, James had to fill out a great deal of paperwork so that Jerry's body could be shipped out of the country. Finally, an official death certificate was issued, with the cause of death listed as a fever of unknown origin.

A hearse met the coffin, once it had landed at the airport in San Francisco. The coffin would be taken to the town of Canaima, where Jerry had lived.

Canaima was a small, aging, but pristine village. By California standards, it was pretty rustic, with church steeples rising up against a background of sun-dappled trees and rambling houses trailing off into the distance.

Once the hearse arrived at the Victorian funeral home, the town undertaker, Irv Kendall, and his assistant, Greg, off-loaded the coffin. They carried it downstairs to the mortuary, where the body would be prepared for burial. It was very dark in the mortuary, the air pungent with the smell of formaldehyde and other chemicals.

Irv set down the ham-and-cheese sandwich he had been eating, pulled the nails out of the coffin lid, and removed it. Meanwhile, his dog jumped up and snatched the cheese out of the sandwich. His cat appeared seconds later and stole the ham.

Irv just stared into the coffin, too shocked to notice the two thefts. Finally, he recovered himself and turned to go to the telephone. With his back to the coffin, he didn't see the first of eight dark, hairy legs poke over the rim of the coffin.

The spider hesitated for a brief second, then

raced down the side of the coffin to the floor below. The room was dimly lit, and the spider darted across the cold tile floor, unseen.

Irv dialed Jerry's parents' house, then waited for someone to answer. "Yes, hello," he said, when someone picked up the other end. "Are Henrietta or Dick available to come to the phone?" He waited, as the person who had answered went to get Dick, Jerry's father. "Dick, hello. Sorry to pester you at this already difficult time, but — I know we'd agreed on an open casket. But — well, maybe we should reconsider. Because — well, because — " He stopped, walking back over to the coffin.

He stared inside, not sure how he should describe the situation.

"I don't know how they work down in South America, Dick," he said finally, "but let's just say their preservation methods apparently differ from ours, and — " He stopped again, looking down at Jerry's badly chewed body — it had clearly been drained of all blood and moisture. Irv shuddered and turned away. "Of course, you're welcome to come down and decide for yourself, Dick," he said, "but . . . in this already difficult time, I really wouldn't recommend — I don't think you should do that. If you understand what I'm saying."

As Irv continued to talk on the phone, the spider moved, swift as a shadow, up the basement steps. Irv's dog and cat bolted out through a small swinging pet door with the spider right behind them.

The spider burst out into the bright sunshine of the cement parking lot.

High in the sky, a blackbird saw the movement and swooped down, hoping for a delicious insect lunch. The bird scooped the spider up in its beak and flew away, wings beating rapidly as it headed for a grove of distant trees.

Suddenly the bird froze in the air — dead — and dropped like a stone through the branches of a large tree, onto the ground in a grassy backyard.

It was a beautiful day in June.

The sun was shining, and Canaima looked pretty enough to be a postcard — a picturesque town square, quaint little shops, large houses scattered along curving streets. The sky was blue, the clouds were white, the trees were green. Canaima looked as safe, and as pretty, as a town could be.

The spider crawled along through the lush green grass. Crickets chirped around it, birds sang, and the grass waved in a gentle summer breeze. It was a perfect day for a picnic.

For the spider, it just might be the perfect day for another little snack. And a little revenge.

The spider stopped, focusing on a beautiful back yard. A moving van was parked in the driveway, and men were unloading furniture and carrying it into the old two-story house. A woman and her eight-year-old daughter were just pulling up in a station wagon, followed by a man and a boy in a BMW. Clearly the family was just moving into their new home.

To the spider, it looked like a nice place to make a new home, too.

Chapter 5

Dr. Ross Jennings parked his BMW behind his wife Molly's station wagon. Ross was in his mid-thirties. It had always been his wife's dream to move to the country, where their children could grow up with fresh air and sunshine.

He and Molly had two children: Shelley, who was eight, and Tom, who was seven. Tom was the first one out of the car when he saw his softball fall out of a carton. The ball rolled away. Tom ran after the ball, hunting for it in the tall grass, unaware that there was a very large spider out there, too.

The rest of the family climbed out of the two cars. Molly was in her early thirties, bright and attractive — and determined to make this change in lifestyle work. She and Ross stood together, looking at the house — and at all of the boxes they were going to have to unpack.

"Okay, kids, go stake out your rooms!" Ross said.

Shelley dashed ahead to the house with Tom right behind her.

"Ross, smell that air," Molly said, taking a deep breath.

Ross also took a deep breath and immediately began to sneeze in an allergic fit. Then he stopped and winked at his wife.

"Very funny," she said.

He nodded, heading for the house, but she pulled him back.

"Let's just — before we discover what valuables broke in the move, and that the breakfront doesn't fit in the dining room . . ." She paused. "Let's just chant, twice: 'We did the right thing. We did the right thing.' "

"For the kids," Ross said.

"For us," Molly said. "For all of us."

Ross nodded. "Good-bye, crime. Good-bye, grime."

Molly nodded, too. "Right." She reached over to take his hand, and they started for the house.

"Good-bye, culture. Good-bye, friends," Ross said.

"Ross, this entire town is yours," Molly said. "You're *the* doctor. Can there be a more respected figure?"

Ross grinned. "Respect is fine, but actually, I've always wanted to be *feared*." Then he noticed one of the moving men casually heft several wooden cases from the back of the truck. "Whoa, careful with that!"

The mover, who was hot and tired, just looked at him.

Ross lifted a bottle of wine from the top case and

examined it. "Whew!" he said. "Good." He looked slightly embarrassed. "Don't, uh, want to agitate the sediments."

"Right," the mover said, and picked up the cases.

"Chateau Margaux," Ross explained. "A hundred twenty-seven bucks a bottle."

"Tasty, huh?" the mover said, and rolled his eyes.

Ross shrugged. "At that price, who can afford to drink it? It goes in the basement."

"Right," the mover said, and he carried the cases away.

"I meant, 'the cellar,'" Ross said to himself, as Molly went ahead of him into the house. "'The wine cellar.'" Pleased with the sound of that, he looked over at the cellar, which had storm doors. "Better get a big padlock — protect my investment."

"Dad!" Tom yelled, running out of the house. "Dad, come quick!"

Ross caught him just before they collided with each other. "Whoa," he said. "What is it?"

"Behind the boxes!" Tom pointed. "Dad, a spider!"

Ross did not look enthusiastic.

"It came *at me*. It was *ugly!* And bigger than this!" Tom demonstrated, with his hands, the huge dimensions of the spider.

"Okay, okay. Calm down," Ross said, leading him back into the house. "Let's find that spider — and let's find your mom, to take care of it."

Tom nodded, pulling him towards the living room.

"Honey?" Ross called. "We're in the living room. We need you to kill a spider."

Shelley ran downstairs. "Kill a spider?" she said. "Cool!"

Molly came in from the den, brushing dust from her hands. "It's bad luck to kill a spider in a new house," she said.

Ross kept his distance as Tom rummaged behind the boxes, looking for it.

"You, uh, you just made that up, dear, didn't you?" Ross said.

Molly gave him a pitying pat on the arm, then advanced towards the boxes, holding a paper towel. "Okay," she said. "Where is it?"

Tom pointed. "Here!"

It was a good-sized brown spider — but certainly not the one from South America. Gently Molly picked it up in the paper towel.

"Poor thing," she said. "It's much more scared of us than we are of it."

Ross looked much less convinced of this than she did.

Molly moved towards the front door with Shelley and Tom right behind her, and Ross significantly farther behind.

"Let's give it a home in the barn," Shelley suggested.

Molly nodded. "Good idea, Shel."

Outside, the South American spider crawled into the barn. The barn was going to be its home, too.

Chapter 6

"Mom, how come you're not afraid of bugs, like Dad is?" Tom asked, as they all walked out to the barn.

"I'm not afraid," Ross said quickly, "of *all* bugs. Just of — " He stopped, gesturing uneasily towards the paper towel in Molly's hand.

The barn, two stories high with a loft, was crammed with old lumber, used tires, abandoned furniture, and other assorted pieces of junk. It smelled very musty; an old pile of hay moldered below the loft. Sunbeams cut through the gaps in the roof and walls, leaving most of the barn in shadow.

Molly knelt down and carefully released the spider.

"Kids, careful of rusty nails," Ross said, trying to reassert his authority.

"Dad, chill out," Shelley said, and she and Tom started to explore.

They had no idea there was something in that barn that they didn't want to find.

* * *

That night, after the kids were asleep, Ross and Molly went to their rooms to check on them. Shelley and Tom were both sleeping peacefully.

"Except for the incident with that — tarantula," Ross said quietly, "today wasn't as terrible as I'd anticipated."

Molly smiled, closing Tom's door behind them as they went out into the hall. "Poor Ross," she said. "Does *every* spider look like a tarantula to you?"

"No," Ross said. "Some of them look like black widows."

Molly smiled, and they went down the hall to their room.

It was night, and there was a full moon out. They hadn't completely unpacked yet, but all the boxes had been lined up, and there were sheets on the bed. Molly went over to the window and threw it open. The sound of crickets filtered inside.

Ross crossed the room to stand behind her and looked out at the star-filled sky.

"Sure you won't miss being in the thick of things?" he asked.

Molly shook her head. "With all those stars winking at us? And those crickets singing? We *are* in the thick of things — natural things. A whole universe."

"I meant work," Ross said. "Strokes from the boss. Christmas bonuses. Office politics, caffeine, adrenaline . . ."

Molly shook her head and moved away from the window. She plugged in one of their lamps, turned it on, and then started to unpack one of the boxes.

"When I realized my idea of success wasn't power, but was freedom from stress — and that I'd never get that at work, no matter how much I earned — that was the turning point," she said.

Ross nodded, helping her unpack. "Comforting," he said, "to know that one of us isn't concerned about money."

Molly laughed. "We'll be fine. Between my severance pay and all your potential patients, we'll be fine," she said. "When're you meeting with Dr. Metcalf?"

"Monday," Ross said. "The old coot passes me the torch at ten sharp." He turned to look at his wife. "We can unpack in the morning. I have a bottle of Napoleon brandy in the basement — the *cellar* — and we could — "

Molly shook her head. "Ross, I'm exhausted."

"It's very *good* brandy," he said.

She smiled. "Okay. Why not?" she said.

Out in the barn, the big brown spider Molly had released crept around, trying to get oriented to its new environment. This particular spider was a female.

The male South American spider stayed in the darkness, watching as the brown spider passed through a bright shaft of moonlight. It was pleased. The brown spider would be the perfect mother for its children. Slowly it moved towards the other spider.

Chapter 7

The next morning, Ross went downtown to meet with the retiring Dr. Metcalf, the man whose practice he would be taking over. He parked in front of a small, attractive office building in the center of town. There was a brass plaque on the door, which read: SAMUEL METCALF, GENERAL PRACTITIONER.

Ross looked at the plaque, then went inside. The conversation didn't go quite as he had expected.

"I have terrific news," Doc Metcalf said, getting right to the point. "At least for my patients I think it's terrific. Though my wife is less than thrilled."

Ross, sitting on the other side of Doc Metcalf's desk, looked at him uneasily. Doc Metcalf had been the town doctor for three generations and was more than a little set in his ways.

"What's the news, Dr. Metcalf?" Ross asked politely.

Doc Metcalf beamed at him. "I've decided to postpone retirement. I don't know for how long, but . . ."

Ross just stared at him. "But — "

"When I really thought hard about it," Doc Metcalf went on, "I realized, there's only one thing left to do after you retire. And I've seen too many friends do that very thing — just six months, a year, after they gave up their professions."

Ross blinked. "But you — when we spoke just four months ago, you assured me — I thought — "

Now Doc Metcalf's smile was less wide. "I'm not ready to retire," he said firmly. "And if my wife can't rush me into it, *you* sure can't."

Ross just looked at him, then sat back heavily in his chair.

When he left Doc Metcalf's office, he still felt dazed, and he got out to his car just in time to see the town sheriff, Lloyd Parsons, putting a ticket on the windshield.

"Uh, excuse me," Ross said.

Sheriff Parsons barely glanced up. "Gotta feed the meter, pard'ner."

"Yes, well, I — I was just leaving," Ross said, "and I — "

"Little late, though, huh?" Sheriff Parsons said.

Ross was in no mood for this. "I *do* have medical plates," he said through his teeth.

Sheriff Parsons was not very impressed. "Oh. You that new doctor?" he asked.

Ross nodded. "Ross Jennings."

Sheriff Parsons' nod was just as brief. "Sheriff Parsons," he said. "You're a Yale grad, I heard."

"That's right," Ross said.

"Yeah, well — it's just a school, isn't it?" He handed Ross his ticket.

"Now, that's quite enough, Lloyd Parsons," a brisk, elderly voice said from somewhere behind them. Margaret Hollins came bustling over. She was in her late sixties but still as spry as could be. She snatched the ticket from Ross and tore it into little pieces. "A young doctor comes to Canaima, and you write him a *parking* ticket?"

"He broke the law, ma'am," Sheriff Parsons said. "And it's my job to — "

Margaret tossed the scraps of paper high into the air so that they showered down around Ross; then she smiled at him.

"Consider this your ticker tape parade," she said.

Ross smiled, touched by this. "Thank you."

"That's littering, Miz Hollins," Sheriff Parsons said, bending down to collect the scraps.

"Lloyd's been a bully since the fifth grade," Margaret said confidingly to Ross. "I ought to know — I held him back. Walk me to my automobile?"

Ross smiled and took her arm. "Thanks for that swift intervention," he said. "How'd you know who I was?"

"We're neighbors," she said. "Gave you a standing ovation when you arrived. Between you and me, Sam Metcalf only recently gave up leeches."

"He also recently gave up retirement," Ross said wryly.

Margaret nodded. It was a small town, and she had already heard the news.

Ross sighed. "We moved down from San Francisco with the understanding that I'd inherit all his patients," he said. "Now I have none."

They were at Margaret's Bronco wagon now, and she stopped, giving him a big smile.

"No, Dr. Jennings," she said, smiling. "You have one."

When Ross got home, he found Molly unpacking things in the room she was going to use for an art studio.

"Look at this — the light!" she said happily, indicating the windows. "On the sunniest day in the city we didn't get light that just — *bathes* you."

She had already unpacked the easel and a framing table, and now she was working on the darkroom equipment.

"Maybe they'll give me a show in town," she said. "Don't they do that in little towns? In the town hall? 'Molly Jennings: A Retrospective.' Of course, I'll need to take some pictures first, but . . ." She stopped, seeing the expression on his face. "What's wrong?"

Ross let out his breath. "There's good news and bad news. Should we go in reverse order or start with the good?"

"Okay," Molly said. "Let's start with the good news."

"I'm seeing my first patient this afternoon," he said. "A great old dame. Lives just up the road."

"Terrific," Molly said. "And the bad news — ?"

"She's my *only* patient," he said.

Molly frowned. "Your only one today?"

"My only one, period," he said. "Metcalf changed his mind. He's not ready to retire."

Molly stared the same way Ross had. *"What?!"*

Ross shrugged unhappily. "He panicked, I think, is what it is. He's decided that if he retires, he'll lose his zest for life and die within forty-eight hours or something."

"But, he *told* you — " Molly stopped. "We looked in fourteen different towns! We bought a house, you rented an office — what are we going to *do?*"

Ross tried to smile. "Kill him maybe?"

Molly took a minute, absorbing all of this. "Okay," she said finally. "I've got my FAX machine. I'll work part-time from here. A phone and a FAX machine, that's all I need. I'll call my old clients, tell them I'm available part-time. Even with half of my commission, we — "

"We're going to be fine," Ross said. "Like you said."

"With *one* patient?" Molly asked.

Ross sighed. "Maybe I'll get lucky, and all of her systems are ravaged by disease — like having seven patients in one."

"Doesn't sound very lucky," Molly said.

Ross sighed again. "Not very lucky at all," he agreed.

Ross examined Margaret that very afternoon.

"You're fit as a fiddle," he said when he was finished. "Not a single thing wrong with you."

Margaret looked sad. "Oh, Dr. Jennings, I'm sorry."

"Sorry?" Ross laughed. "What did you think, I was hoping you'd have some terrible disease?"

"Well — what about my blood pressure?" Margaret asked hopefully.

"You have above-normal *systolic* pressure," he said. "That's far less dangerous than a disastolic elevation. And yours is well below a level that requires treatment."

Margaret took a bottle of pills out of her purse. "Then I don't need these?" she asked.

Ross looked at the bottle, then tossed it into the trash. "No," he said. "I, uh, I guess Dr. Metcalf isn't aware of the difference between the two types of hypertension."

"I already told you," Margaret said as she got off the examining table, "Dr. Metcalf isn't aware of the difference between his head and a hole in the ground."

Ross laughed.

"But Canaima folks're comfortable with him," Margaret said more seriously. "Wasn't always so, though. When he first hit town, just after the war, everyone was terribly standoffish."

"Really?" Ross held the door for her and walked her out to her car. "How'd he overcome that?"

"He threw a party," Margaret said. "Invited the whole town. If Sam Metcalf was half as good at medicine as he is at public relations — " She shrugged, getting into her car, then paused before starting the engine. "That's it! Next month, when the afternoons are cooler, we'll throw you a party!"

Ross smiled. "We will?"

"We sure will," Margaret said. She winked at him, and drove away.

Back at home, Molly wandered around their new property with her camera, while Shelley and Tom played on the lawn. She took pictures of this and that, ending up at the barn.

She swung open the old wooden door. Dust floated in the shafts of sunlight. She hesitated, then stepped inside. She looked around, her eyes falling on a spiderweb.

This wasn't just any web. This web was very intricate, each strand glistening in the sunlight.

Molly kept staring, then raised her camera to take some pictures. It was like no web she had ever seen.

Chapter 8

That night, Molly cooked a big Italian dinner for the family.

"So, your one patient," she said, serving Shelley some salad, "is she a walking health hazard?"

"She's perfect," Ross said.

"So what are we going to do?" Molly asked.

"We're going to enjoy the fact that since we no longer live in San Francisco, we no longer have to refer to this as 'pasta.'" He sucked in a forkful of linguine with great enthusiasm.

"Skinny spaghetti!" Tom said, and sucked a few strands even more noisily into his mouth.

Ross and Shelley thought this was funny, but Molly was too worried about the state of their finances to be amused.

"On the bright side," Ross said, to cheer her up, "Margaret, my tragically healthy patient, has offered to throw us a Get to Know Dr. Jennings party. One cup of punch with the handsome new GP and the good people of Canaima will see the light, abandon mean, old Doc Metcalf, and everything will be — "

"Well," Molly cut him off, "it's a nice gesture, anyway."

Ross nodded. "I thought so."

From outside the kitchen window, a girl about Shelley's age waved, and Shelley waved back.

"Can we go play with Bunny?" she asked, already halfway out the door.

"I want you in before dark," Molly said.

Shelley nodded and hurried outside, with Tom in hot pursuit.

"Bunny?" Ross said.

"Bunny Beechwood," Molly explained. "She popped over this morning. A neighbor. Seems nice."

Ross smiled. "What do you want to bet they're going to go chase fireflies?"

"With sticks," Molly said wryly, and got up to clear the table.

Ross followed her with a stack of plates. " 'The country.' 'Neighbors.' I have to admit," he said, "if we don't starve to death here, it's all kind of — cute."

"Very cute," Molly agreed, laughing. "I got some great shots in the barn today. If my camera picks up the web with half the detail my eye did — "

Ross froze. "The 'web'?"

Molly nodded. "Our little spider made quite a home. Even *you* would appreciate — "

Ross dumped the dishes in the sink, shaking his head and ignoring the crash. "I don't think you understand, Molly," he said, deadly serious. "I have — "

" — a terrible fear of spiders," she said, finishing the sentence for him. "Which is why you should force yourself to come look at the web."

"Look at the web?" he asked. "Why?"

"To see it for the extraordinary and beautiful creation it is," Molly answered. "Therapy. To work through this irrational — "

"It's *not* irrational," Ross said, irrationally. "My fear derives from a very specific incident."

"I know, darling," Molly said, squirting dish detergent into the sink.

"I was two years old — " he started.

"Nobody remembers anything from when they were two," Molly said, running the hot water.

"*I* do," Ross said. "It's my first memory."

Molly turned off the water and took his hand.

"Come on," she said. "Let me just show you."

He followed her reluctantly to the barn.

"I was in my crib," he said, telling the story even though she had heard it before. "I'd just woken up from a nap. I opened my eyes — and there it was. Probably just a daddy longlegs, but . . ." He shuddered at the recollection.

Molly led him across the yard.

"It seemed just *huge*," he said, "and it came crawling through the bars of the crib, and it touched my bare leg. I was only wearing a diaper — and all my limbs just froze in fear. As though I were *paralyzed*. I couldn't stop it as it crawled along my skin. I distinctly felt all of its legs, and — " He had to swallow, hard. "Then, it came up to my face, and — the feeling of utter helplessness, of being *explored*, by this alien *thing*, I — can you *blame* me for being a spiderphobe?"

They were at the barn now, and Molly opened the door.

"Arachnophobe," she said.

"Whatever," he said. "It was the worst — " He stopped, catching sight of the web.

It *was* oddly beautiful — huge, delicate, and complex.

"Impressive, isn't it?" Molly said.

"I think you spared the eight-legged Frank Lloyd Wright," Ross said, moving a little closer. He took a step towards the ladder that led up to the loft. "Therapy, right?"

"What courage," Molly said, grinning. "My hero."

Ross started climbing the ladder to get a closer look at the web. "Therapy," he said quietly. "Therapy."

He climbed higher and higher, closer and closer to the web, while Molly watched from below.

"See?" she called up to him. "You still have full use of all your limbs."

Near the top of the ladder, Ross paused, his smile stiffening when he saw cocooned insects and half-devoured mouse carcasses trapped in the web. He gulped, took a step backwards, and lost his balance. He grabbed at one of the ladder rungs.

The wood was rotten, and the rung gave way. The vibrations knocked part of the web loose and something came flying down on a web strand right towards Ross's face. It was a dead rat, its head in a hangman's noose of webbing. It bounced off Ross and then dangled there, jerking slightly as though it were still alive.

Ross made a sound that was very much like a scream, then fell off the ladder and landed in the moldy hay below. Molly, who was also screaming, helped him up, and they both ran out of the barn and slammed the door behind them.

High above them, in the loft, there was a white silk egg sac. It was a spider-egg sac. Small gray spiderlings were climbing out of the sac by the hundreds.

They were hatching.

One spider emerging from the egg sac was much bigger than the others. The South American spider immediately pushed it away from the other spiderlings. A queen had been born.

Chapter 9

It was a month later, and Margaret was having her party for Ross. It was a lovely, cool late-summer afternoon. Children played on Margaret's lawn, while the town's social power circle gathered around the table of hors d'oeuvres on the patio to greet the Jenningses. Doc Metcalf, along with his wife, Evelyn, were among the group.

"I've done some checking on you, Ross," Doc Metcalf said, his voice stern. Then, he turned to face the others. "When I'm finally ready to throw in the towel, Dr. Jennings is your man. By all accounts, a fine physician."

Ross and Molly managed weak smiles.

"This sure brings back memories," Doc Metcalf said, popping a cheese ball into his mouth. "Right after the war, when I moved to Canaima, the whole town threw me a party."

"No, Sam," his wife said. "You threw yourself a party."

Doc Metcalf ignored that. "Now *that* was a party," he said to Ross and Molly. Then he took his wife's hand and led her towards the stuffed mushrooms.

"Now *that* is a jerk," Molly whispered to Ross, who smiled.

A big, friendly looking man came over to Ross a few minutes later.

"Mayor Bob Blacknell," he said, jovial as can be. "Canaima welcomes you."

Ross put out his hand to shake, but the mayor was busily unbuttoning his collar. Then, he pulled his shirt out, exposing a large, ugly birthmark on his collarbone.

"Think I should have this removed?" he asked.

Ross handed him a business card. "Here," he said. "Come see me at the office."

"Oh, no," the mayor said. "Sam Metcalf's my doctor."

Ross nodded solemnly, then looked at the birthmark. "Sure hope he gets all of it," he said, and walked away.

Molly was stuck with the Beechwoods — big, strapping father, Henry; his huge teenage son, Bobby, both with matching buzz cuts; his pretty daughter, Becky; and his wife, Edna. They were all watching the youngest Beechwood, Bunny, leading Tom and Shelley in an energetic game.

"What's that Bunny's showing them?" Henry asked.

He squinted over at the children, then smiled. "Green Beret hand-to-hand combat techniques," he said.

"Oh." Molly looked at the Beechwood teenagers.

"So, uh, Becky, have you thought about what you'll major in at college?"

"Gym," Becky said briefly.

Henry grinned proudly. "It's in the genes," he said. "Bobby here's the Titans' star quarterback. Taught him to throw a football before he could walk. I coach the team."

"Ah," Molly said, trying to be polite. "Nepotism?"

Henry looked blank.

"Actually," Edna said, "we're Baptists."

"Oh," Molly said, and managed a polite — if dazed — smile. "How nice."

Back in the Jenningses' barn, the South American spider brought a freshly killed cricket up to the hayloft. The little spiderlings had grown up. They were a new breed, with the distinctive waspish shape and markings of their father.

These days, the spider was kept very busy, catching food for its offspring, nourishing them for the strenuous mission ahead.

The spiderlings were always very, very hungry.

At the party, Ross and Molly had retreated to the privacy of the punch bowl. Ross poured a cup for each of them. They each took a sip and then gasped.

"Pace yourselves," Margaret said, coming up behind them. "That's my high-octane, no-knock premium blend."

"Packs a punch," Ross said weakly.

Molly, who was still trying to catch her breath, just nodded.

After finishing their lunch, the spiderlings began to crawl single-file down a post that supported the hayloft. They crawled down to the pile of hay and then headed for the barn doors. They moved in little columns, like crack soldiers. Once they got outside, they fanned out in several directions.

They were ready to start their mission. They were ready to get revenge.

Back at Margaret's house, Ross and Molly were now standing with Irv and Blaire Kendall — the mortician and his wife. The Kendalls had yet to leave the hors d'oeuvres table, and they had eaten more than their share. They were still eating.

"Nobody comes up to a mortician at a party and says, 'Irv, buddy, y'don't think I might be dead, do ya?' " Irv said, with his mouth full. "Must drive you nuts, trying to dip a chip while somebody shows you his growths."

"Drive you nuts," Blaire said, and had another piece of shrimp toast.

"You know," Ross said, trying to change the subject, "until quite recently, my wife was a successful stockbroker."

Irv looked at her. "How about that. You hear about the new Artificial Intelligence lab, just went public, up in Palo Alto?"

Before Molly could answer, a voice near the punch bowl caught everyone's attention.

"Why *shouldn't* I have another?" a woman asked, her voice slurred. She had just poured herself a cup of high-octane punch, and her husband was trying to get her to put it down. "No!" she said, yanking her hand away and spilling part of the drink. "I'm *thirsty*."

Tactfully Ross and Molly looked away. The Kendalls did, too.

"The Manleys," Irv said. "Their son passed away recently."

"That's awful," Molly said. "How?"

Irv shrugged. "Not sure. He was a photographer — caught something on some scientific expedition in Venezuela."

The Manleys were Jerry's parents — and his mother was very drunk.

"Have you ever lost a son?" she asked the party in general. "I'll stop right now for anyone who ever lost a son." She refilled her punch cup. "And nobody'd tell me how he died or even let me see him to say good-bye. What's *happening* to this town?"

Below the table, in the grass, the first of the spider soldiers had arrived. It crawled up the table leg and then scurried across the tablecloth. Nobody saw it.

Margaret came over to help Jerry's father, and the two of them led Jerry's mother away from the table. She dropped her cup in the process and it landed upside down, on the spider. Nobody noticed the cup moving — apparently, by itself — across the table. Then the cup fell into the grass.

Jerry's mother was crying now, and Margaret

helped her into the car, while Jerry's father got behind the wheel.

"I had to recommend a closed coffin," Irv said guiltily, watching all of this. "The body looked chewed up — like some vampire'd had a go at it."

Nobody knew what to say.

When the party was finally over, Ross, Molly, and the Kendalls were the only ones left. Ross and Molly went over to say good-bye to Margaret, and to thank her.

"I wager you made enough friends today to break Sam Metcalf's death grip," she said, smiling.

Ross smiled back. "It was wonderful, Margaret. I can't thank you enough."

"Nor I," Margaret said, "for freeing me from those damn pills. With my system clean, I feel like I could compete in a triathalon."

"On the basis of your checkup, I'd tend to agree," Ross said.

He and Molly headed for the car, leaving the Kendalls behind. Irv and Blaire each helped themselves to one last meatball.

"Irv? Blaire? Can I get you a doggie bag?" Margaret asked cheerfully.

The Kendalls nodded with great enthusiasm.

Once she had packed them up some leftovers, Margaret went inside and closed her door. She didn't notice the spider that had followed her.

Chapter 10

Before she went to bed, Margaret put her cat, Felix, out for the night.

"Happy hunting, Felix," she said. "See you in the morning."

She locked the door and then carried her nightly glass of milk into the living room. She set it on an end table, in front of a framed photo of her late husband.

"You'd've drunk too much punch and been the life of the party," she said to the photograph, smiled, and started sipping her milk.

Just above her, there was a large, dark moving shadow. It was a spider — hiding inside the lamp shade. Margaret didn't notice and continued sipping her milk.

She set the empty glass down on the table and pressed a light kiss on the photo. Then she pulled the chain of the lamp to turn it off. The spider, with a soft hiss, dropped onto her wrist.

* * *

The next morning, Ross was down in the wine cellar, assembling a wine rack. The wine rack was from a kit, complete with directions, but he was still having a little bit of trouble. Finally he put down his screwdriver.

"Ta-da!" he said, to no one in particular. "For my *next* trick . . ." He picked up his nail gun to attach the wine rack to the ceiling.

The nail shot right through the ceiling as though it were made of cottage cheese, not wood.

Upstairs, Molly was just hanging up the phone, while Tom played with toy cars on the floor. A nail broke through the floor in front of him, blocking the car's path.

In the cellar, Ross looked up at the ceiling in some confusion and fired another nail. It shot up through the floor, almost going through Molly's foot.

"Ross!" she shouted.

Ross ran upstairs, looking very upset.

"I'm sorry," he said. "I could have killed one of you — the nail just went straight up. It's all rotten down there. Probably *crawling* with termites. I'm surprised we haven't fallen through the floor!" He frowned. "My poor wine cellar."

"I'll call the exterminator," Molly said vaguely.

"*You're* rather casual about the death of my dream," Ross said.

Molly nodded. "I've been trying to reach Margaret to thank her for last night. The line's been busy all morning."

"Then I guess she's gabbing," Ross said, with a shrug. "Old ladies are known for gabbing, right?"

"Go check on her," Molly said. "Please?"

"Sure," Ross said, shrugged again, and headed for the back door.

Once he was outside, he walked briskly towards Margaret's house. Halfway there, he began to get an ominous feeling, and he broke into a run.

When he got to her house, he found her cat scratching at the door — and her newspaper lying in the driveway, uncollected. He frowned and picked both of them up.

He carried them up to the door and peered inside. There was a light on in the kitchen, even though the room was filled with sunlight. He frowned again and moved to another window, looking inside at the living room.

The telephone was on the floor with the receiver lying two feet away. Even more uneasily, Ross moved to the next window.

Inside, he saw Margaret's foot sticking up. It wasn't moving.

Doc Metcalf, Sheriff Parsons, and Irv Kendall and his hearse all arrived within a few minutes of each other. Ross sat on the porch, dazed and disbelieving.

"Whaddaya think, Doc?" Sheriff Parsons asked Doc Metcalf, after all of them had gone inside to examine the body.

"Heart attack," Doc Metcalf said grimly. "Bound to happen sooner, rather than later. She had a history of high blood pressure. Even with the pills I'd put her on — "

"I took her off them," Ross said, dully.

Doc Metcalf glared at him. "What right did you have to do *that?*"

Ross sighed. "She came to me," he said. "As a patient. I examined her, and — "

"You didn't see that she was hypertensive?" Doc Metcalf demanded.

"Her diastolic reading was normal," Ross said, very tired. "Her systolic elevation was below one sixty. If you've stayed current, you know that's not considered — "

"This is a very serious matter, young man," Doc Metcalf said huffily, moving aside as Irv and his assistant carried Margaret's body out of the house on a stretcher. "You may well have killed this lovely woman."

Ross shook his head. "I don't think so. She was in fine shape. I want an autopsy."

"*Never,*" Doc Metcalf said.

Ross pressed his teeth together, trying not to lose his temper. "She was my patient," he said calmly.

"And mine, for forty years," Doc Metcalf said. "God knows Margaret wouldn't want to be butchered. Nobody in this town would want that for her. You come from a big city, where people don't care about each other. I don't expect you to understand, Doctor."

Sheriff Parsons nodded. "That's right. That's sure right."

"Give it here, Lloyd," Doc Metcalf said to him.

"I'll sign the death certificate myself."

"I'm satisfied if you're satisfied," Sheriff Parsons said, handing him the papers.

Swiftly Doc Metcalf signed them, then frowned at Ross. "A little advice, Doctor," he said. "If you're ever going to fit in here in Canaima, you'd better learn to be sensitive to the feelings of the good people here."

"Sorry," Ross said. "I'm more interested in medicine than public relations."

Doc Metcalf scowled at him and headed for his car.

"Cardiac victims don't usually bite their tongues in half like that," Ross said after him. "It's as though she went into tetanic convulsions. Until I know why, this case isn't closed."

Doc Metcalf spun around to face him. "You're damned right it's not closed," he said. "I believe that you may be guilty of malpractice. I intend to pursue the matter to its conclusion." He got into his car, slammed the door, and drove away.

Ross just stood there, watching him go.

The funeral was held two days later. The skies were gray, as most of the town gathered at the cemetery. After the service was over, Henry Beechwood, the football coach, came over to Ross.

"I understand she was your patient," he said. "Your only patient."

Ross nodded grimly.

"Come by the gym tomorrow, at three," Henry

said. "I'll throw some business your way."

"Thanks, Henry," Ross said, coming up with a tired smile. "Thanks a lot."

That night, Ross sat unhappily in the living room. Molly came in and sat next to him on the couch.

"She was young," he said. "To die at sixty-eight. That's ten years below the life expectancy of a Caucasian female, did you know that?"

Molly put her hand on his arm. "Ross, you're a fine doctor," she said. "I'm sure you knew exactly what you were doing when you took her off those pills — "

"Like I knew what I was doing when I chose this town? With the doctor who wouldn't quit?" he asked. "Or this fine house? Which is rotting from the ground up?"

"I'm going to take care of that in the morning," Molly promised. "The exterminator is coming over."

"Yeah, well, Margaret's still going to be dead in the morning," Ross said, and then set his jaw. "And I still want to know what killed her."

Chapter 11

Bright and early the next day, a pickup truck pulled up in front of the Jenningses' house. An enormous insect with wild bloodshot eyes and drooling jaws was painted on the side of the truck. Below the insect was the motto: "Bugs Be Gone. McClintock Infestation Management."

Delbert McClintock stepped out of the truck and swaggered towards the house. He was a large man who took great pride in his exterminating expertise and his state-of-the-art hardware.

As Molly went to let him in, Delbert stopped in the doorway and sniffed the air.

"Termites, huh?" he said, wisely.

"That's what my husband thought," Molly said, nodding.

"Uh-huh." Delbert sniffed again, wisely. "He's an expert in these matters?"

"Well — no," Molly admitted.

"Didn't *think* so." He stepped into the house. "Glad you called me. No room for amateurs in this game."

Molly brought him over to the cellar door. Half-way down the steps, Delbert stopped and whipped out a stethoscope. He placed it against the wall, then listened intently.

"What is it?" Molly asked, fascinated in spite of herself.

Delbert frowned. "Hard to say for sure. Would anyone object if I tore down this wall?"

"I would," Molly said.

Delbert shrugged. "False alarm, then. Lead on."

Once they were downstairs, he used the flame from the furnace lighter to see behind the furnace.

"You've got humidity down here, from being close to the river," he said, very solemnly. "Guess you know that moisture and a nice steady temp are Miami Beach for your basic termite."

"I didn't know that," Molly said.

Delbert nodded. "Didn't think you would." Then, he saw a can of commercial insecticide stored on a nearby shelf, and he chuckled. "Won't find that *that* helps much." He poked around some more, then frowned.

"How bad is it?" Molly asked, by the stairs.

"Didn't find a one," Delbert said, and frowned again. "Go figure."

Molly frowned, too. "Then why is all the wood rotting?"

"I'll tell you why," Delbert said. "Bad wood."

"Okay." Molly nodded, not sure how to approach that. "So, what should we — do?"

Delbert shrugged. "Tear out the bad wood. Put

in good wood." He walked around the wine cases and peered inside.

"My husband thought this would make a good wine cellar," Molly said.

Delbert nodded. "I collect beer cans, myself." He started back upstairs to the kitchen. "Got a rare '74 Miller Lite. Misprint on the label. Only a hundred or so cans in circulation. Your husband might just want to take a gander."

"I'll, uh, I'll pass that along," Molly said, and showed him to the stairs leading to the second story.

After careful examination of the second floor, Delbert got a ladder and poked around underneath the eaves, where he found a nest.

"Wasps!" he said triumphantly, then chipped the somewhat decayed nest free. He looked at it in great disappointment. "Gone now, though." He climbed down the ladder. "But they'll return — bet on it. So before they do, let me recommend a program of preventative foomigation."

" 'Preventative foomigation?' " Molly repeated, not sure if she had understood his pronunciation.

Delbert nodded, happily. "See," he said, "in relation to the insect world, I'm cruel. Vengeful, even." He paused. "But my rates are reasonable."

"Okay," Molly said, "but how can you 'foomigate' what isn't here?"

Delbert sighed a very deep sigh. "It's hard to explain this to a nonprofessional."

Molly took his arm and steered him downstairs. "I'll bet it is," she said.

Over at the high school, Ross followed Coach Henry Beechwood across the gymnasium.

"I know what a blow losing Margaret was for you," Henry said. "People keep score, and you're only as good as your last game. Hey, I oughta know *that*, right?"

Ross nodded. "I appreciate your concern, Henry."

"Well, I want you to enjoy Canaima," Henry said, slinging a big arm around Ross's shoulders. "Clean water, fresh air, and instead of police sirens wailing all night, you've got crickets. Crickets up the wazoo."

"Actually," Ross said, frowning, "I haven't heard any crickets lately. Now that you mention it."

Henry stopped walking. "Actually, I haven't, either," he said.

They frowned at each other, then continued walking over to the line of teenaged boys to whom Ross was going to give physicals.

Later, Ross sat outside in the football-field bleachers, watching the Titans scrimmage. He had nothing better to do. There were a few other spectators, including some cheerleaders, and Henry stood on the sidelines, yelling at his players.

"You're not Titans, you're turkeys!" he was shouting.

In the meantime, a gray spider — one of the spiderlings — was crawling along the top of the grandstand behind Ross. It spun a single thread of web and swung down to the next row, ending up behind two girls with blonde hair.

The girls were giggling while they watched the football practice, blissfully unaware that death lurked mere inches, and seconds, away. Feeling something, one of the girls reached back to touch her hair. But, it was nothing — maybe just the wind.

The spider spun another long thread and drifted down to the ground. It began crawling over towards the team's bench.

"That was supposed to be a banana out?" Henry yelled at his players. "Looks more like a banana split!" He turned back towards the bench. "Miller! You know these patterns?"

Todd Miller, a scrawny senior, looked up from his feet on the bench. "Better than the back of my hand, sir!" he called back.

"Then get out there and show me!" Henry said, jerking one thumb in the direction of the field.

Todd picked up his helmet, not noticing the spider that had just crawled inside. He put the helmet on, fixing the strap as he ran out to the field.

As the quarterback called the play, Todd felt something funny inside his helmet. Before he had a chance to check it, the ball was in play. He ran out to catch a long pass and was immediately tackled and buried by a pile of other players.

Gradually all of the Titans got up from the pile and limped away. Except for Todd, who was lying still on the ground.

Henry came over to see what was wrong. "Give

him air, boys," he said. "Give him air. You all right, Miller?" He rolled Todd over to check him more closely.

The spider was on the ground where Todd's helmet had been, and as Todd's concerned teammates came over, the spider was squashed beneath someone's cleats. They all stared — stunned — at their vacant-eyed teammate.

"Oh, no," Henry said quietly, then straightened up, cupping his hands to his mouth. "Hey, Ross! Come quick!"

Ross was already running across the field. But it was too late.

Chapter 12

And so, once again, the townspeople had to gather at the cemetery for another unexpected funeral. After it was over, a group of concerned parents gathered around Doc Metcalf.

"From what I heard," Doc Metcalf said grimly, "it wasn't a very hard tackle. I only wish I'd known. You see, Dr. Jennings examined him last."

Ross, on his way to his car with Molly, overheard this. Quickly, he ducked inside to avoid the stares of the anxious parents.

When he and Molly got home, they were tired and depressed. Shelley and Tom were on the front porch, waiting for them.

"What's wrong, kids?" Ross asked, trying to sound cheerful.

Tom and Shelley looked at each other; then Shelley spoke up.

"Bunny Beechwood says that everyone's calling you 'Doctor Death,' " she said.

Ross flinched, taking a step backwards.

"Well, that's just silly," Molly said quickly.

"*And* they say you wanna cut people up in little pieces," Tom blurted out, "and then . . ."

Ross sighed and sat down on the porch next to his children.

"It's called an autopsy," he explained. "It's not a pleasant thing, but sometimes it's the only way you can find out what happened to a person." He moved his jaw. "But some doctors, who should know better, just won't accept that."

It was nice and cool that night, and the Metcalfs had the window in their bedroom opened wide to let in the cool breeze. Doc Metcalf was on his treadmill, briskly walking in place.

"Some doctors who should know better just don't accept that," he was saying. "Their big-city methods don't sit well in a small town."

His wife was in bed, reading. "Both Margaret and that poor boy *did* seem to be healthy," she said. "A bit odd, don't you think, Sam?"

Although neither of them could see it, there was a very large spider under the bed.

Doc Metcalf shrugged, dialing in a calorie count on his treadmill. "If I autopsied everyone who died of a heart attack," he said, "I'd be run out of Canaima so fast . . ."

The spider moved out from underneath the bed and scuttled along the edge of the treadmill machine. It paused, then leaped up at Doc Metcalf's leg.

The spider missed, landing, instead, on the moving belt, and was swept back between Metcalf's feet. It went around twice on the belt before losing its grip and being knocked onto the carpet.

"You're not jealous of our new young doctor, are you?" Evelyn asked.

"What?" Doc Metcalf said grumpily. "Now I've lost my rhythm."

"Come to bed, Sam," Evelyn said.

Doc Metcalf, very cranky by now, shut off the machine, then sat down on the edge of the bed and took off his shoes and socks.

The spider seized this moment to dart inside Doc Metcalf's slipper.

"I need to shower," Doc Metcalf said, and started for the bathroom.

"The tile's cold," Evelyn reminded him.

Doc Metcalf sighed, but slipped his feet into his slippers. He took one step, then shouted in pain.

"Ow!" he said, yanking his foot out of the slipper.

"What's wrong?" his wife asked.

"Some stupid thing *bit* me," he said, hopping on one foot as the spider ran away, into the safety of the shadows under the bed. Evelyn just barely caught a glimpse of it.

"Oh, no!" she gasped. "It was a spider."

"A spider?" Doc Metcalf said grumpily. "It felt like a *cougar!*" Then, as the toxins began to reach his nervous system, he grabbed his chest. "I — I'm having a heart attack," he said weakly.

He sank down to the floor, hyperventilating and perspiring heavily. Evelyn sprang out of bed in a panic and bent down next to him.

"Sam!" she said frantically. "What should I do?"

"C-Call an ambulance," Doc Metcalf said, his voice rasping. "And Jennings, and . . ." He doubled up in pain as he began to convulse.

Ross and Molly were just getting ready for bed when the phone rang. Ross answered it.

"Hello?" he said. "Yes, Mrs. Metcalf — yes! Of course!" He grabbed for his shirt, putting it back on. "Stay calm. I'll be right there!" He slammed the phone down and ran out of the room.

Molly raced after him. "What's going on?"

"Metcalf — he's having a seizure!" Ross yelled, and ran out of the house.

Once again, he was too late.

Chapter 13

This time, along with the police and an ambulance, Ross put in a call to the county medical examiner, Milton Briggs, who arrived at the scene shortly thereafter.

When Briggs got out of his car and headed for the Metcalfs' back door, Sheriff Parsons moved to intercept him.

"You didn't have to come here, Milt," he said.

"I'll be the judge of that," Briggs said, and headed inside. "Wait out here — guard the house or something."

The medical examiner went into the house and upstairs, where Doc Metcalf's limp body was lying on the floor of his bedroom. There was blood at one corner of his clenched lips.

"Was he alive when you got here?" he asked Ross, who was also in the room.

"No, he'd been dead maybe five minutes," Ross answered. "Whatever it was, it was abrupt and acute."

Briggs nodded, studying the body. "What's your guess?" he asked. "Massive coronary or cerebral hemorrhage?"

Ross hesitated. "His wife said that he was bitten by a spider just before he had the seizure."

Briggs looked at him for a long minute and then smiled. "Oh, right," he said. "Sam told me about you. You're the new hotshot MD who won't accept anyone else's diagnosis."

"I'll accept it if I agree with it," Ross said defensively.

Briggs nodded. "Good."

Ross bent down next to the body. "I'd like to show you something." He pointed at Doc Metcalf's foot, where there were two red dots: tiny puncture wounds spaced close together, the width of a large spider's mouth. "I believe that's a spider bite there."

Briggs squinted at the marks, then nodded. "I'll buy that," he said. "But I rather doubt that's what killed him. In twenty years, I've seen only one spider-bite fatality, and that involved a black widow and a one-year-old child." He got up, looking at the treadmill. "My guess is that Sam overexerted himself. Did you check the treadmill setting? The dial was up near max."

Ross looked at the dial, sighed, and followed Briggs downstairs. Evelyn Metcalf was in the kitchen, being comforted by the Metcalfs' three grown daughters.

"You may be right," Ross said quietly, before they went into the kitchen to see her. "I know the spider thing sounds crazy. I just want the chance to definitely rule it out."

Briggs nodded, stepping out onto the back porch to summon the medics to come take the body away.

"I'd like a full autopsy," Ross said. "Tissue samples, blood toxicology, the whole nine yards."

Sheriff Parsons, standing nearby, overheard this. "Now just wait one second," he protested. "Here in Canaima, we — "

"Be quiet, Lloyd," Briggs said, then turned to Ross. "You'll get Evelyn's permission, of course."

Ross nodded.

"Okay, then." Briggs started down the back steps. "You take care of yourself, now. You're the town doctor."

Ross nodded, numbly. This was not the way he had wanted to get the job.

Back at the barn, the spider and his queen carried a new egg sac outside. The weather was getting cold, and it wanted to find a warmer place for its children. It squeezed through the Jenningses' ground-level basement window and disappeared into the wine cellar with the egg sac.

The next day, Ross's office was filled with patients.

"They'll have to be removed, right?" an anxious mother said, as Ross examined her little girl's throat.

Ross shook his head. "No," he said. "We'll treat the inflammation with antibiotics."

The mother looked surprised but relieved. "When my son had this, Dr. Metcalf put him right in the hospital," she said.

"Well." Ross started writing out a prescription, choosing his words carefully. "Until fairly recently, tonsils were thought to be useless. First sign of infection, yank them. Now we realize their presence helps the immune system."

"So I don't get to have ice cream?" the little girl asked, very disappointedly.

"I'll buy you a double-scoop on the way home," her mother promised, and they left the office.

Ross had a very busy day with patients — a new experience for him in Canaima — and he was tired after work, but he stopped off at the library on his way home.

"Sure," the librarian said, when he asked. "We have a few books about spiders. Wait here; I'll get them."

She bustled off, returning shortly with several books, including a children's book, *The Very Busy Spider*.

Ross handed that particular one back to her. "Thanks," he said, smiling, "but I already have this one."

The librarian looked disappointed but checked out the others for him.

"Thank you," Ross said.

"Certainly," she said. "I hope you find what you're looking for."

Ross kind of hoped that he *wouldn't* find it.

Chapter 14

The books were not terribly helpful, so the next morning Ross started making some phone calls. It was very hard to hear over the noise of Molly washing the breakfast dishes, and Tom and Shelley playing with the prize they had gotten out of the box of cereal.

"Well, then, can you transfer me to your science library?" Ross said, on the telephone. "Thank you."

While he waited for the transfer to go through, Tom and Shelley kept playing with the toy — which happened to be a black rubber spider.

"Oh, yes," Ross said, when the science library answered. "I'm looking for research on domestic spiders and fatal shock reactions in human bite victims." He listened briefly, then sighed. "Okay, then, can you transfer me to your *medical* library? Thank you."

While he waited, again, Shelley sneaked over and planted the rubber spider on his wrist. Ross looked down impatiently and then froze.

"It's just pretend, Dad," she said. "It can't hurt you."

"Remove it," Ross said, tightly.

Shelley quickly picked up the rubber spider, and Ross started breathing normally again.

"Mom, are there really killer spiders in Canaima?" Tom asked.

"I sure don't think so, honey," Molly said, and then looked at Ross, tapping her watch to indicate that he was going to be late to work.

Ross nodded and quickly finished his phone call. Once he had hung up, Molly walked him out to the car.

"Honey," she said, very mildly, "do you think this 'theory' of yours might just be a product of your own arachnophobia? And that you're needlessly spooking the kids?"

"Maybe," Ross said. He started the car. "Meanwhile, make sure they don't play near that old barn."

Molly sighed, but nodded, and Ross pulled out of the driveway. Then Molly turned to see Tom and Shelley playing with a Frisbee toy — right in front of the barn.

"Kids, would you please play in the house?" she said.

"Why?" Shelley asked.

"It's going to rain," Molly said.

Tom looked up at the bright blue sky. "When?"

Molly sighed again. "Sometime. Please just come inside, okay?"

Tom and Shelley looked sulky but followed her into the house.

Ross's office was as crowded as it had been the day before, and when Ross hurried in, his new receptionist — Doc Metcalf's old receptionist — looked up impatiently.

"I know," Ross said. "Sorry, Janice — I promise to be on time from now on. And I promise to treat you as well as Dr. Metcalf always did."

Janice smiled tightly. "Frankly," she said, "I was hoping for better."

Before Ross could start examining any patients, the phone in his office rang. It was Milton Briggs, the medical examiner.

"Okay, hotshot," Briggs said. "Are you sitting down? According to the preliminary data, Sam Metcalf died as the result of a minute amount of an as-yet-unidentified toxic substance in his bloodstream. My office isn't ruling out accidental poisoning, deliberate poisoning — or even killer spiders. At the moment, it looks like cardiac arrest to me, but I'll support whatever you'd like to do."

Ross nodded, digesting all of this. "Thanks, Milt," he said. "I'm going to ask that the other bodies be exhumed. I've got to be sure."

"Okay," Briggs said. "You've got my support."

"Good," Ross said. "I think I'm going to need it."

At lunchtime, Ross went over to Sheriff Parsons' office. The sheriff's reaction was less than enthusiastic.

"Are you out of your mind?" he said, staring at Ross from behind his desk.

"Let me say it again, more slowly," Ross said, trying not to lose his temper. "I want Margaret Hollins' and Todd Miller's bodies exhumed."

Sheriff Parsons looked blank.

"Dug up," Ross said.

Sheriff Parsons shook his head firmly. "Hey, you start pulling citizens out of the ground," he said, "who should be enjoying their eternal rest, and all of those patients you lucked into will disappear so fast, you'll — "

"If I have to," Ross interrupted him, "I'll get a court order. Milt Briggs is on my side."

Sheriff Parsons frowned at him but he sat down. "This is a bad business, Mr. Big-City Doctor," he said quietly. "A very bad business."

Ross nodded grimly. "That's what I've been trying to tell you," he said.

Chapter 15

When Ross got home that night, Molly was saying good-bye to Shelley. Worried to see his daughter getting into a strange car, Ross rushed over.

"What's going on?" he demanded.

"Shelley's going to spend the night with Bunny," Molly said calmly.

"Oh." Ross blinked. "Oh."

"We'll take good care of her, Dr. Jennings," Becky Beechwood said from behind the wheel.

"Wait a minute." Ross leaned into the car and looked at Shelley and Bunny, who were sitting in the backseat. "There may be spiders around that can be very dangerous. I want you girls to be aware of this. If you should see one, don't try to kill it or capture it. Just run. Understand? *Run.*"

Shelley and Bunny giggled. Nervously.

"We'll be sure to do that, Dr. Jennings," Becky said, none too impressed. " 'Bye now."

As Becky drove away, Molly patted Ross's shoulder. "You've had a long day, haven't you?" she said.

Ross nodded. "Very long," he said.

At the Beechwoods' house, Bunny and Shelley went up to Bunny's room to play. They changed into their pajamas and sat on Bunny's bed, surrounded by Bunny's dolls and stuffed animals.

"The eensy, weensy *spider*," Bunny sang, and they both giggled, "went up the water spout."

They both giggled wildly, neither of them noticing a large gray spider with strange markings scurrying across the ceiling to the overhead light, right above them.

"Down came the rain," Bunny sang, "and washed the *spider out!*"

They both screamed in a blend of terror and sheer delight.

The spider started to spin a web thread, one end of which was attached to the overhead light.

"Little Miss Muffet sat on her tuffet, eating her curds and whey," Shelley said. She lowered her voice dramatically. "Along came a — *spider* — and sat down — *beside* — her!"

They both screamed again and laughed.

The door flew open. Becky stood there with her hands on her hips.

"If you girls don't settle down," she said, "then Shelley can't stay over anymore."

The spider, halfway down the thread, scrambled back up and out of sight.

"We can't sleep," Bunny said.

Shelley nodded. "We keep scaring each other."

"Well, come on," Becky said. "Why don't you two sleep in my bed for a while."

"What about you?" Bunny asked.

Shelley picked up one of the dolls from the bed — a doll with a strand of web attached to it.

"I'm going out," Becky said. "I have a date."

"*You* have a date?" Bunny said, and laughed.

The spider began to swing back down the strand, towards the doll in Shelley's hand. Just as it was about to reach the doll, Shelley shut Bunny's bedroom door behind her, squashing the spider in the door. The spider landed on the floor with a thump.

Shelley had no idea how close she had been to death.

It was late, and Ross sat under one light in the dark living room, poring over the reams of spider information that had been sent to the house over Molly's FAX machine during the day, from universities and research institutes all across the country. Most of the papers were highly technical reports, filled with repulsive diagrams and unintelligible statistics.

Ross read each one very carefully, highlighting pertinent passages as he went along.

A small, dark shape was moving across the window ledge. It came closer and closer — and then hopped right onto Ross's hand. He flinched.

It was only a cricket. A harmless, frightened-looking cricket that had somehow wandered into the house. Gently Ross picked the little insect up and looked at it.

"So, tell me," he said softly, "where are all the other crickets? What happened to them all?"

The cricket was silent. So was the country night.

Ross set the cricket down and went back to his notes. Over and over, the same name kept coming up — a professor named James Atherton. Clearly he was the most prominent expert in the country. And he was located in California.

Now Ross knew where to start the next day. He straightened up the pile of notes, then got up and turned off the light.

"Good night, cricket," he said. "Take care."

But the cricket was already gone.

The next morning, Becky took her time with her morning shower, monopolizing the Beechwoods' bathroom. Her father knocked sharply on the door.

"May I have some privacy, please?" Becky said.

"There are other people in this house, young lady," her father said sternly.

"I'll be out in a minute," Becky said. She turned on the water.

As Becky shampooed her hair, she didn't see the web connected to the showerhead and the tile wall. The force of the water knocked the web free, right on top of her hair. Becky just kept shampooing, not even feeling it.

The spider who had spun this web jumped angrily on top of Becky's head and perched precariously on top of a hank of hair. Becky brushed the hank of hair back, and the spider fell onto her nose.

She screamed — louder than Bunny and Shelley

could ever have screamed, but before the spider could bite her, the force of the water spray knocked it off her body and towards the drain.

Still screaming, Becky leaped out of the bathtub.

The spider righted itself, and climbed up the wall and out of sight.

Becky just kept screaming. She didn't know where the spider was, but she was sure that it was coming back.

Chapter 16

After rushing upstairs to calm his daughter down, Henry rushed right to the telephone and called Delbert, the exterminator.

Delbert's pickup truck pulled up in front of the house about an hour later and, carrying many more tools than seemed necessary, Delbert stomped into the house and upstairs.

"See this?" He showed Henry his asbestos glove. "You need an asbestos glove. Doomsday weapon in Delbert's war on creepy-crawlies. I coat it with PD-4, the insecticide with an environmental conscience. It's biodegradable, organic, and you oughta *see* the tiny beasties twitch when they get so much as a *whiff* of the stuff."

"There's a rumor going around town that some kind of spider killed Sam Metcalf," Henry said as Delbert bent down to feel around behind the toilet. "Maybe Margaret, too. Maybe even my ballplayer."

"Doubtful, Henry," Delbert said, feeling around. There *was* a spider back there, but it was expertly avoiding Delbert's glove. It actually seemed to be enjoying itself. "There was a case in Florida," Delbert went on, "where one of my colleagues bumped into a nest of black widows — sustained a dozen bites and lived." He straightened up, having found nothing. " 'Course he permanently lost control of his bodily functions."

"Of course," Henry said.

Delbert looked around vaguely. "No spiders here," he pronounced. "*But*. I'm going to hunt down the alleged arachnid, Henry, and — I'm going to spritz him from here to eternity!" He nodded to punctuate that, and then went down the hall to start searching the bedrooms.

Ross, tired from his late night of studying, sat in his kitchen in front of an untouched breakfast of bacon and eggs, talking on the phone.

"Yes," he said. "Could you transfer me to Dr. Atherton's extension?"

"It's eight-thirty," Molly said impatiently. She was getting a little tired of Ross's new spider fixation. "Nobody's going to be there yet."

"If he's half the fanatic I think he is, he will be," Ross said. "In fact, I wouldn't be surprised if — Oh, hello. Dr. Atherton?"

"Yeah, this is Atherton," James said, sitting in front of a large terrarium in his Cal Polytech Research Lab. "How can I help you?"

"This is Ross Jennings," Ross said. "I'm a general practitioner, downstate. I have a problem that may be spider-related, and you seem to be the foremost authority on the West Coast — or, uh, any coast, and — ”

“Look,” James said. “Jennings, is it? Every so often there is a health scare in some little town somewhere. An unexplained outbreak. And spiders make convenient culprits. Men mistrust any creature with more than four legs. We’ve all heard the myths, the horror stories — but did you know that on every acre of your town there lives an average of fifty to sixty thousand spiders?”

“No,” Ross said. He didn’t like the idea much, either.

“And,” James went on, “did you know that each spider eats about a hundred insects per year? That adds up to at least five million insects consumed per acre, annually. Consider, Doctor, that man might find the planet uninhabitable without spiders.”

“Dr. Atherton.” Ross sighed. “I have nothing against spiders.”

Molly, listening to his end of the conversation, laughed. Ross motioned for her to be quiet.

“But there’ve been three deaths in my town,” he said to the professor, “and I’m afraid there’ll be more. If you could just lend me your expertise for an afternoon — we’re not all that far, a town called Canaima — ”

“Canaima?” James interrupted.

“Yes,” Ross said. “Are you familiar with it?”

“Well, the name seems — ” James stopped, trying to remember why he had heard of “Canaima.” Then he gave up. “Anyway. Let me see what I can do. Where are you, exactly?"

Ross flashed Molly a thumbs-up sign and gave the professor directions.

After hanging up the phone, James went to the outer lab to see if he could recruit someone to go to Canaima for him. He was too busy to go — most of his research time these days was spent studying the two South American spiders he had brought back alive.

He found two young assistant professors playing a spirited game of Foosball among the sinks and vivisection tables. He cleared his throat, and the game immediately stopped. The two professors looked sheepish.

"Collins," James said to one of them, "are you going to be *equally* busy tomorrow?"

"Uh, no," Collins said. "Don't think so, sir."

"Good," James said. "I want you to do a favor for me."

Delbert was still searching the Beechwoods' house for spiders. He had just finished checking the crawl space, with no success.

"Crawl space's clean, too," he said. He pulled the trapdoor shut.

The two spiders on the top of the trapdoor clung to the wood to keep from being knocked off.

"So what do we do?" Henry asked as Delbert climbed down off his ladder.

"I'll answer that in two words," Delbert said. " 'Preventative foomigation.' "

Henry sighed. "Well, you're the expert."

Delbert grinned. "And don't you forget it," he said.

Delbert went outside to get the "foomigation" equipment from his truck. He stopped short, seeing an odd-looking gray spider, right there on the front steps. Delbert whipped out a can of insecticide like a six-shooter and squirted the spider, drenching it before it could run away.

"There," he said, satisfied. "*That'll* fix you." He started to put the insecticide back — and the spider began to crawl away.

Somehow, it was still alive.

Delbert stared at the spider, amazed. Then he swiftly stepped on it, stomping it into nonexistence.

Delbert frowned, looking at the squashed mess. "Hmmm. Better uncork my private stock," he said aloud. "These little suckers may be tougher than I thought."

Chapter 17

The next day Ross, Medical Examiner Briggs, and Sheriff Parsons went to supervise the exhuming of the bodies at the cemetery. Irv Kendall and his assistant stood nearby, watching the gravediggers at work. Nobody looked very happy, but Sheriff Parsons looked *miserable*.

A taxicab pulled up, and Chris Collins, the assistant professor of entomology, got out. He didn't look very happy, either.

Ross went over to him. "Dr. Atherton?" he asked.

"Chris Collins," Chris said. "One of his assistants."

"Oh," Ross said. He shook Chris's hand, somewhat disappointed.

"Atherton's extremely busy these days," Chris explained. "He recently discovered a new species of spider in South America. To us, it's a big deal."

"Well, I hope you can help," Ross said, and gestured over his shoulder. "We're going to be exhuming some bodies."

"Hey," Chris said, and looked sick. "Sounds like a blast."

When the bodies had been recovered, they were taken straight to Irv Kendall's mortuary to be examined.

"We're looking for bite marks," Briggs said to Chris, who nodded uncomfortably.

Ross pointed out the marks on Doc Metcalf's foot. "Like these," he said.

Chris leaned forward to look and then shuddered.

"A spider did this, right?" Ross said.

Chris shrugged uncertainly. "I'm not sure," he said. "I think so, but anyway, even at several times the potency of *Latrodectus* — "

"That's the black widow?" Ross guessed, remembering the name from his reading.

Chris nodded. "Right. Even then, it'd take more than one bite to kill. So I have to assume that this man's death and the spider bite — if it is a spider bite — are coincidental."

Ross and Briggs didn't answer as they examined Margaret's and Todd Miller's bodies. Irv Kendall stood nearby, mournfully munching from a bag of potato chips.

"Poor Margaret," he said. "She was a good wife, good teacher, good neighbor." He sighed profoundly. "And an *excellent* cook."

"I think I need some fresh air," Chris said, heading for the door.

"Wait a minute." Ross pulled him back, having located the bite marks on Margaret's wrist and arms. "You still think it's a coincidence?"

Chris swallowed but looked more closely at the marks.

"I don't know," he said finally. "These *could* be spider bites. The tissue surrounding the bites is macerated."

The word "macerated" rang a bell with Ross, and he frowned, trying to remember when, and where, he had heard it, in reference to this case.

"Found them," Briggs said, as he examined Miller's body. "One mark on his neck. One behind the left ear."

Chris let out his breath. "I need to make a phone call," he said.

"Right this way," Irv said, and led him upstairs.

Chris dialed the lab at the university and explained the situation to James.

"So I think you'd better come down here, right away," he finished. "I think it's for real."

"All right," James said, after a pause. "I'll be there tomorrow. Find me a specimen, okay, Chris?"

"I'll try," Chris said, but he knew that it was going to be like looking for a needle in a haystack.

He went back downstairs to join the others, only to find Ross and Briggs on their way over to see the mayor.

"Sheriff here'll run you out to a nice motel and bill the town," Ross told him. "Tomorrow, we'll meet at the Metcalf house and find one of our non-existent spiders."

"Hey, I'm no chauffeur!" Sheriff Parsons said indignantly. "I got law and order to maintain. Why can't *you* drive him, Doc?"

"Milt and I are going to see the mayor," Ross said. "He's going to have to go on television, warn the town."

"You're going to panic everybody!" Sheriff Parsons yelled.

"That's the idea!" Briggs yelled back.

Mayor Bob was not very receptive to the news about the spiders, nor to the idea of warning everyone.

"Very, *very* interesting," the mayor said, sitting in his living room, not sounding very interested.

"So, you'll make an announcement?" Briggs asked.

"That's something I'm going to look into, Milt," the mayor said, nodding. "Very, very carefully."

"It would need to be done quite soon," Ross said, as tactfully as possible. "We can help you write it, if you — "

"That would be helpful, sure," the mayor said. "And I thank you for offering. Whether or not I can take you up on that offer is dependent on a host of other factors."

"Like what?" Ross asked.

The mayor shrugged. "I have to get into that with my people. ASAP. Just know that you two are now very, very much in the loop."

"Bob?" the mayor's wife called from the kitchen. "Suppertime."

"Ooops!" the mayor said. He stood up, beckoning for his guests to do the same. "Suppertime.

Shouldn't you boys be home with your families?"

"But we really have to — " Briggs started.

The mayor ignored that and showed them to the door. "Families," he said. "When you get down to it, they're what make a town worth saving." He smiled at them, then closed the door.

Ross and Briggs stood there, looking at each other.

"He's a 'kinder, gentler' mayor, huh?" Briggs said.

Ross nodded. "My hero," he said.

Ross had a lot of trouble sleeping that night. He lay in bed, with Molly peacefully asleep beside him. Ross kept his gaze moving around the room, looking for spiders, looking for anything out of the ordinary.

Then he saw one.

He grabbed a magazine from his night table, rolled it up, and slipped out of bed, moving across the room to the wall where the spider was. He whacked it, hard, but nothing happened. Probably because it wasn't a spider at all — it was a picture hanger.

Feeling foolish but relieved, he turned to go back to bed. Then, he heard a light tap-tap against the window. The headlights of a passing car projected the silhouette of spider legs, furiously waving, tapping at his window.

Ross crept over there, the magazine shaking in his hand, to make sure that the window was shut tight, to make sure that — but it wasn't a spider at all. The "tapping tentacles" were merely twigs of the branch of a tree just outside.

Now Ross felt *really* stupid. He started back over to his bed — and stopped. There was a spider slowly creeping across the floor. Huge, ugly, terrifying — it wasn't a spider at all! It was a dust ball, being blown along by the draft from an air vent.

Ross let out his breath, then slowly put the magazine down. Obviously he wasn't going to get any sleep tonight.

He went downstairs — the insomniac arachnophobe — to watch some television. He sat down on the couch in the den, remote control in hand.

The first channel was airing a commercial for Raid. He changed it and heard a *Saturday Night Live* spoof of Spider Sabitch." Ross changed the channel to the movie *The Incredible Shrinking Man*. The movie just happened to be at the scene in which the hero battles a spider. A very big spider.

This wasn't working out.

Ross frowned and changed the channel in time to hear the announcement: "Stay tuned for *Dragnet*, with Jack Webb." He changed again. This time, he heard an announcer's voice saying, "Tomorrow at nine, the network premiere of *Cocoon*." Ross gritted his teeth and changed the channel again, finding the fifties science-fiction movie classic *Them*, in which the good guys are forced to battle giant ants.

Ants. Ants weren't as bad as spiders. Ross put the remote down.

He watched intently as the heroes fought the big

insects with flamethrowers, and the ants began dying in great, fiery explosions. "Burn, baby, burn." Ross muttered to the TV.

In the movies, everything always seemed to work out.

Chapter 18

The next morning, Ross went over to meet the others at the Metcalfs' house. He was very tired.

Sheriff Parsons arrived last, with the house keys. He also looked tired and grumpy.

"Perk up, Lloyd," Ross said. "If we find the spider that did this, you can arrest him."

Sheriff Parsons just looked at him and unlocked the front door. Ross went inside, with Briggs and Chris Collins right behind him. The house was quiet and still — Doc Metcalf's wife had gone to stay with relatives.

"Milt, why don't you cover the living room," Ross suggested. "Chris, check the dining room. Lloyd, take the kitchen. And I'll, uh, oversee the operation. Sort of, you know, *coordinate* things."

Sheriff Parsons went out to the kitchen and straight to the pantry, helping himself to a box of cereal. He sat down at the table and began to eat the cereal right out of the box. He didn't want to find a spider any more than Ross did.

Chris was the first to locate something. He found a web between the house and the above-ground cellar doors outside. He immediately called Ross, who joined him outside. The web was heavy with repulsive bits and pieces of it-was-hard-to-say-what.

"What *is* all that junk?" Ross asked, standing back a ways.

"Leftovers," Chris said, studying the bits more closely. "I'd guess mostly cricket parts — wings and legs. Spiders love crickets."

"You know, it's, uh, it's kind of funny," Ross said, not finding it funny at all. "No one in Canaima has heard any crickets these past few weeks."

He and Chris exchanged uneasy glances.

Inside, Sheriff Parsons was enjoying his snack. But just as he reached his hand into the box to get some more, he saw a spider inside. He shouted, dropped the handful of cereal, and leaped away from the table in shock and surprise.

The others came running.

"It's dead," Chris said, getting there first.

"What could've killed it?" Briggs asked.

"The shock of seeing Lloyd?" Ross guessed.

Sheriff Parsons was the only one who was not amused.

So they kept searching the house, even more carefully. Briggs crawled along the floor in the den, inspecting the cracks in the floorboards, while Ross lifted an inch of the rug up with the toe of his shoe. Lifted it *boldly*.

"Couldn't we just pack up the dead spider and get out of here?" Ross suggested.

Chris, about to look behind a painting, laughed. "Why?" he asked. "God's little vampires giving you the willies?"

Ross frowned. "Why vampires?"

Chris shrugged. "Spiders drain their victim's fluids," he said. "Just a joke."

But Ross wasn't smiling. "This trip of Atherton's," he said slowly. "To find the new spider species. Where did he go?"

"Venezuela," Chris said, lifting the bottom of the painting away from the wall.

A spider leaped out at his face, missed, and landed on the carpet. Ross jumped even farther back than Chris had.

"Is that — one of them?" he asked.

"Looks like a mighty fine suspect," Chris said, reaching for a large crystal ashtray on a nearby end table. "Would you step towards it, please?"

Ross shook his head firmly. "Chris, I'm — scared to death of them."

"We all are," Chris said, shrugging. "But our brains secrete a neurotransmitter that helps us deal with — "

"I, uh, I don't have that particular neurotransmitter," Ross said.

"Yes, you do," Chris said. "Everyone does."

Ross took a deep breath and then a small step forward. The spider whirled in his direction, giving Chris a chance to slip behind him and drop the ashtray, trapping the spider, which lunged furiously against the glass.

"Can it get out?" Ross asked uneasily.

"I sure hope not," Chris said.

Professor Atherton arrived a few hours later, meeting Ross at his office.

"Did you find me a specimen, Doctor?" he asked, after they had exchanged introductions.

Ross nodded. "Yes," he said. "Then, I paid a call to the town mortician. Several months ago, there was a corpse — Irv had never seen anything like it. The body was desiccated, totally drained of blood."

James shrugged. "So what?"

"Irv's feeling is that if a big enough spider spent a long-enough time working on that body . . ." Ross shrugged to indicate the probable results.

"So" . . . James was puzzled. "You think . . ."

"I think that's why you've heard of Canaima," Ross said. "This was Jerry Manley's hometown."

James blinked. Twice. Then he recovered himself.

"He was our photographer," he said. "He died in camp — of fever, we assumed." He nodded, seeing the expression on Ross's face. "I know. One should never assume."

Ross nodded. "I think one of your Venezuelan spiders hitched a ride here in Manley's coffin."

"That, uh, that sounds like a reasonable hypothesis, Doctor," James said. "Now, let's pray that you're wrong."

They went into Ross's examining room, where Chris and Briggs were waiting. Chris had set up the table for dissecting, complete with scalpels, tweezers, a magnifying cup, a glass cutting board, and various other tools of the trade.

The live spider had been placed in an old empty fish tank, with heavy mesh over the top. James bent down to peer through the glass.

"It looks like a relative of the *Olias*," he said. "But it's quite a bit bigger." He tapped on the glass with one finger, and the spider lunged at it.

James straightened up, frowning. "That isn't a good sign," he said. "We'd better test the strength of its venom."

James had brought a few laboratory mice along, and he set their cage to one side before beginning the dissection of the spider. First, he suffocated the spider with rubbing alcohol.

There were three green sacs mounted near the spider's fangs.

"The fangs, the injectors, are disproportionately large," James remarked. "Three *huge* poison sacs." He inserted a hypodermic needle into one of the sacs, withdrawing the contents.

Ross and Briggs watched with mingled fascination and revulsion. Chris was just plain fascinated.

"Judging by the fangs and the reservoirs," James said, "I'd estimate a deliverable dose would be a quarter cc." He injected ¼ cc of the toxin into one of his mice.

They all waited to see what would happen.

"You see," James said, ever the professor, "in a

venomous bite, both the type of toxin and the amount injected determine the effect. That, and where the bite is. It may paralyze, or it may kill."

He set the mouse back down in its cage. The mouse blinked, ran in a circle, and then squeaked. It fell over — perfectly normal one second; dead the next. A small amount of blood appeared at one corner of its mouth. Exactly the way the blood had appeared on each of the human victims.

Ross broke the stunned silence. "Look, I'm no expert," he said, "but I'd guess that this toxin is fatal at a fraction of that dose."

James nodded very slowly. "You'd be right," he said.

Chapter 19

After another long minute of silence, James walked over to the microscope where the dead specimen from the cereal box had been placed. He peered through the lens.

"That's odd," he said. "They have no sex organs."

"Wow," Chris said. "That would make them like drones or soldiers. It's typically seen in highly organized insect societies — bees or ants — but I've never seen it before in spiders."

James looked grim. "I have."

"Venezuela, right?" Ross said.

James nodded. "This is a descendent, all right," he said. "Somehow, a South American male must have mated with a common house spider and produced a very deadly strain."

"But if it has no sex organs, then it can't reproduce, right?" Ross asked.

"Right," James agreed. "And its accelerated growth and specialization suggest that its life cycle is probably quite short."

"We *found* that one dead," Chris said.

"Good," James said, and looked through the lens. "That's the silver lining in this situation."

"Okay," Briggs said, speaking up for the first time. "Now let's discuss the cloud."

"Okay," James said and thought briefly. "In their own ecosystem, the species I discovered is at the top of the food chain, interdependent with one another — conscious, even. They radiate from the central nest in a weblike pattern and dominate the entire area. In their original habitat, they were contained by geography. That's not true here."

There was another silence.

Briggs looked at Ross. "I understood all of that."

Ross nodded. "Absolutely," he said. "Me, too."

The door opened, and Sheriff Parsons came in with Delbert, the exterminator.

"Excuse me," Sheriff Parsons said, keeping his eyes away from all of the dissection equipment. "Professor, this here's our town exterminator. He believes he came across one of the offending spiders only yesterday."

"Yup," Delbert said, and stuck out his hand. "Delbert McClintock, Infestation Management. Always a pleasure to meet a colleague."

"Did you bring the spider?" James asked, ignoring his hand.

"Actually, it's probably still on the bottom of my shoe." Delbert lifted a heavy-booted foot to look. "Nope. Can't really tell what it is anymore. Sorry." Then he grinned. "So what're we spritzing, and where?"

James turned back to Ross and Briggs, to continue his explanation.

"The male has created soldiers," he said. "It has probably produced a new queen. The new queen, when mature, will eventually create reproductive offspring. If that happens, this town might be nothing but dead. Then, the next town. And so on."

"What would it take to stop all of this?" Ross asked.

James shook his head, completely stumped.

"I think *this* might convince 'em to cease and desist." Delbert held out his asbestos glove. "Asbestos. *Drenched* in PD-4. The five fingers of death."

Ross picked up the phone and dialed the mortuary. "Manley's body was brought to Irv's mortuary, so that's where the infestation must have originated. If we can get in there and destroy the original male — "

"And/or the primary nest," James said, nodding.

Ross frowned at the phone. "It's busy."

Sheriff Parsons checked his watch. "*Wheel of Fortune*, Doc," he said. "Irv and Blaire always take the phone off the hook during *Wheel of Fortune*."

"Then let's get over there," Ross said, hanging up the phone and heading for the door.

"I'm going to call the Department of Agriculture," James said. "Alert them to what's happening here." He pointed at Sheriff Parsons. "You'll drive me over, right?"

"I'm the sheriff!" Sheriff Parsons said. "Not someone's chauf — "

Everyone else just looked at him, and he subsided.

"I'll go to the mayor's house, about quarantining the town," Briggs said, going to his car. "And this time, I'm not asking — I'm telling."

"We'd better hurry," Ross said to Chris and Delbert. "I hope we're not too late."

Irv and Blaire were having a fine time watching *Wheel of Fortune* and eating microwave popcorn. They loved microwave popcorn.

During a commercial, Irv went out to the kitchen to make more.

"Blaire?" he shouted over the volume of the television. "Real butter or fake?"

"Real!" Blaire yelled.

While Irv was getting the butter, a spider crawled into the popcorn bowl. Irv melted the butter in the microwave, poured it over the popcorn, and carried the bowl out to the living room.

Blaire was on the couch, and he snuggled up next to her to watch the rest of the show. They loved *Wheel of Fortune* even more than they loved microwave popcorn.

Delbert drove like a wild man over to the Kendalls' house — while Ross and Chris clung to the dashboard.

"What'll the nest be like?" Ross asked, as they sped along.

"If you found it, you'd know it," Chris said. "The

room'd be dark. Moist. There'd be a musty smell. You'd see an egg sac."

"Like, you know, your *basic* egg sac," Delbert said, not very helpfully.

"Right," Chris said. "White, cocooned, pulsating. About the size of a baseball."

Ross nodded, trying to commit all of this to memory.

Back at Ross's office, James wasn't having much luck getting through to the head of the California Department of Agriculture.

"Yes," he said through his teeth to the person at the other end of the telephone. "I expect you to interrupt your boss's dinner party. *Please*." He listened briefly, then slammed the phone down. "They'll be 'getting back' to us," he said to Sheriff Parsons. "I should be out at the mortuary, not — " He shook his head and left the office, going through the waiting room.

He stopped, seeing some of Molly's photographs on the wall. There were pictures of San Francisco, of a house, of two children, of a barn. And there was a picture of a very large spiderweb, with a distinctive, intricate pattern.

"Do you know where this is?" James asked, pointing at the picture.

"Sure," Sheriff Parsons said. "It's the old Daniels place. Ross Jennings bought it."

James looked at the picture some more, and then looked very worried.

"I think you'd better take me there," he said.

* * *

At the Kendalls' house, Ross banged fiercely on the front door knocker, but nobody answered.

"Can't hear us over the television," Delbert said.

Chris reached forward and found the door unlocked. He looked at Ross, who shrugged.

"Canaima welcomes you," Ross said.

Swiftly they went inside.

On the television, Vanna was applauding a winner. The studio audience was also applauding. The Kendalls were sitting together on the couch.

"Irv," Ross started, "We have an emergency, we — " He stopped.

The Kendalls were very still. The Kendalls were very dead.

Chapter 20

Over at the Jenningses' house, Sheriff Parsons had just pulled into the driveway. James jumped out of the car before it even stopped. He was carrying Parsons' powerful police-issue flashlight and a large collecting jar.

He hurried over to the barn, opened the door, and swept the flashlight beam around. He was looking for something. Then he found it — the web.

"There it is," he said, very calmly. "Please go to the mortuary and round up my assistant. And that exterminator."

Sheriff Parsons was happy to leave. "I'll do that," he said. "Meanwhile, you wait out here, sir. I can't be responsible if you — "

"You just go along," James said, and went into the barn.

He swept his flashlight beam from left to right, all across the barn floor. The beam picked up the tiny reflective eyes of a handful of soldier spiders, watching. James was not interested in the soldiers.

"Where are you?" he said softly. "I'm going to find you."

He stepped onto the bottom rung of the ladder and began climbing to the loft. Climbing higher, he saw that the web was even bigger than it had appeared, extending up into the rafters. The lower portion was heavy with captive prey.

"My, my," James said. "You've been a busy boy. . . ."

In the loft, his eyes caught the silken thread spiders always used as a "trip wire," a thread that would vibrate when something was caught in the web, signaling the spider in its hideout above. Very lightly, with the flashlight, James tapped the trip wire.

"Supper's here," he whispered. "Come and get it."

Up in the shadows, the South American spider peered down with its ruby-red eyes. It was not as stupid as this man thought. It would not be so easily fooled.

James kept gently touching the trip wire with the flashlight, holding the collecting jar in his free hand. Apparently, the spider wasn't coming.

With a sudden gasp of forboding, James whirled to see — the bright ruby-red eyes. The spider jumped at him. James screamed. The flashlight fell from his hands to the hay below.

Then, it was very quiet.

* * *

Ross and the others searched the basement mortuary but didn't find the nest. They came back outside, discouraged, and maybe a little afraid.

"The nest *had* to be in there," Ross said. "Where else could — ?"

"Wait a minute," Delbert said, reaching back inside through the window they had broken to get in.

Ross and Chris waited, eagerly.

Delbert brought his hand back out, clutching a jelly doughnut that had been on the counter. He smiled and took a big bite out of it.

"It'd been in there, I'd've found it," he said, still chewing. "Finding nests is what I'm all about." He nodded twice and ambled over to the pickup truck.

"Delbert, do you have a map of this town?" Chris asked.

Delbert took one out of the glove compartment. "Thinking of buying here?"

"I get it," Ross said, catching on. "What Atherton said, the spiders . . ."

". . . radiate out from a central nest," Chris said, finishing the sentence. He pulled out a pen and handed it to Delbert. "Where was Irv's house? Mark it!"

Delbert shrugged and put an X on the map.

"And the old guy," Chris said. "The doctor."

Ross leaned over the map, making an X of his own.

"The football player?" Chris asked.

"Died on the football field," Ross said. "Behind the high school."

Delbert marked the spot. "That'd be right here," he said. "This is kind of fun."

Chris ignored that. "What about the first victim, what was her name?"

"Margaret," Ross said.

Delbert marked her house on the map. Then Chris connected the four marks, forming a diamond.

"Okay," he said. "In the middle there. Is that the mortuary?"

Ross looked at the map, then closed his eyes. "No," he said. "It's a house."

"Well, who lives there?" Chris asked impatiently.

"*I* do," Ross said.

Chapter 21

They drove down the dark country road at top speed, Ross frantic with worry.

"The barn!" he said over and over. "Of course! It's the barn! I'm so stupid — Molly, the kids — the whole time, the nest was in my barn!"

"I frankly doubt that," Delbert said, sharing some exterminator wisdom. "Your basic spider'd find your old barn a tad breezy this time of year. In that respect, spiders're a bit like you and me. No, the nest's not in the barn."

Ross gritted his teeth. "Just *drive*," he said.

Back at the mortuary, Sheriff Parsons was knocking on the door. He knocked and knocked.

"Hello?" he called. "Hello in there? Delbert? Anyone? Yoo-hoo?"

Nobody was there to answer.

Delbert swerved into Ross's driveway, and Ross jumped out of the truck.

"I'm getting my family out," he said. "Destroy whatever's in the barn."

"Well, now, could we barter this one, Doc?" Delbert asked. "See, sometimes, when I cough, I — "

Ross wasn't even listening. "Chris, there may be spiders in the house," he said.

Chris looked from him to Delbert, not sure which way to go.

"You licensed to be present at a Level Four foomigation?" Delbert asked.

Chris looked at Ross. "Let's go," he said.

They ran to the house, while Delbert moved — calmly, purposefully — to the barn.

He opened the door and stepped inside, surprised to see a flashlight — still on — lying on the floor.

"Hmmm," Delbert said. "Hello?"

There was no answer.

He took it one step at a time, spritzing soldier spiders right and left.

"*Got* one," he said. "Got *two*." He blew imaginary smoke from the end of the spray gun and started up the ladder.

Halfway up, he stopped — there was a fallen board in the way. He pushed the board a little and then James's head, wrapped in a silky cocoon helmet, dropped right in front of his eyes. Spiders busily crawled in and out of it.

Delbert stared. "Whoa!" he said, and backed swiftly down the ladder. Looking up, he could see James suspended, upside down, in the giant web.

"They got the doc!" Delbert said. He switched

on the spray gun. "All right, you little monsters —
let's see who's uglier, you or me!"

And then, he started spraying poison like there
was no tomorrow. There was, after all, a good
chance that there wouldn't *be* a tomorrow.

Ross and Chris cautiously entered the house, not
wanting to walk into a trap — or scare Molly and
the children.

"Honey?" Ross called, his voice shaking a little.
"Molly?"

"Ross?" Molly's voice floated out from the den.
She sounded very calm. "We're in here."

Ross and Chris looked at each other and moved
slowly towards the den, scanning every surface they
passed. There were no spiders to be seen.

Molly and the children were sitting on the couch,
watching television.

Molly looked up from the book she was reading,
clearly annoyed. "I expected you home for dinner,"
she said. "I was worried — I called the office and
you weren't there."

Ross didn't answer as he scanned the room.
There was a spider on the drapes and another one
on the wall.

"Hi, Dad," Tom said cheerfully.

Ross walked into the room, taking measured,
deliberate steps. "I want you all to get up very
slowly and move towards the door," he said.

"But, Dad," Shelley protested, "the show's not
over yet."

Just then, a spider crawled across the television screen.

"Go!" Ross ordered, pushing them towards the door, towards Chris, who guided them safely out of the room.

On the wall, behind the television, there was a geometric pattern of — something. Now the "pattern" scattered. It was a pattern of spiders.

Ross herded the family to the front door. But where there had been no spiders a minute ago, there were now half a dozen, patrolling the door and door handle, blocking their escape.

"Upstairs," Ross said urgently.

A spider dropped from the ceiling onto his jacket, and he swatted his hand against the inside lining, knocking it off.

"Go on!" he said. "We'll climb down from the roof!"

They ran upstairs, with spiders following right behind them. More spiders dropped down through cracks in the old ceiling. Ross ushered everyone into the upstairs bathroom and slammed the door.

Then Chris saw the gap underneath the door. "Quick," he said to Ross, "they'll come in under there!"

The two men grabbed bath towels and kicked them tight underneath the door. Then, Chris took a breath and turned to the rest of the family.

"Hi," he said. "I'm Chris."

Behind him, two spiders rattled loose the plate surrounding the door lock. They pushed it free, climbed into the bathroom, and raced down to the tile floor.

Molly grabbed a towel and dropped it over them. She crushed one with her foot, while Ross jumped on the other. Chris snatched a wad of tissues and stuffed them into the keyhole. But, none of them saw a *third* spider run across the back of Shelley's T-shirt and head for her bare arm.

Tom saw it and reached for Ross's can of shaving cream, squirting wildly. The spider dropped to the floor, entombed in a glob of foam.

Chris threw the window open and looked outside.

"All clear," he said. "Come on!"

Ross hoisted Shelley out to the roof. Molly did the same with Tom.

"Climb down the trellis," Molly said. "I'm right behind you."

There were small thuds as spiders hurled themselves at the door, trying to get in.

"Go!" Ross said to Chris.

He helped Chris out the window and was about to follow when a spider jumped on his leg. Ross shook it off, then stepped on it. The spider was still alive, and he kicked it. It landed at the base of the door, and Ross kicked again, with such force that the lower panel of the door came away and a horde of spiders streamed into the room.

He would never make it to the window in time. He was surrounded.

Chapter 22

Chris was just starting down the trellis when it pulled away from the side of the house and collapsed under his weight. He hit the ground hard, and Molly rushed over to help him.

Shelley and Tom screamed, pointing as a swarm of spiders headed for Chris, who was lying helpless on the ground. He was doomed.

There was a sudden glare of light, and the spiders stopped. It was the headlights on Delbert's truck and he stood silhouetted in front of them, fresh insecticide canisters strapped to his back.

"Rock and roll!" he yelled, spreading spider death and destruction in his path.

In the bathroom, Ross crouched up on the sink. He could see that the trellis had broken, and that there was no way down. Meanwhile, the spiders had started to climb *up*.

Ross ran out of the bathroom — spiders began dropping from the ceiling.

He started down the stairs, grabbing the banister for support. But there was a spider on the banister, lying in wait.

Ross violently flailed his arm to throw it off, which sent him careening backwards against the railing — which splintered and tore away from its supports.

He was falling. He toppled fifteen feet to the floor below, still clutching a piece of banister. The force of the fall sent him crashing towards the cellar stairs. His weight broke the heating duct, and he fell through it, landing on the cellar floor, debris covering him.

The rug and floor lamp from the room above him also tumbled through the hole, the lighted lamp swinging upside down, still plugged in.

In the dim lamplight, Ross looked around frantically, expecting to see as many spiders as he had seen upstairs — the spiders he had barely escaped. He flailed his arms wildly to defend himself, but then realized that there were no spiders in the cellar at all. He was alone.

Confused, he looked up at the gaping hole above him, dust and debris still filtering down. The cellar was very quiet and, except for the swinging lamp, very dark. The air was moist and humid — almost musty.

There was a huge egg sac attached to a post in the cellar's annex, but Ross didn't see it. Neither did he see the queen spider, as she spun a long, silken thread and swung down to the annex floor. She climbed over the annex's sill and into the cellar, making her way towards him.

Ross looked around, then sucked in his breath. "Dark, moist, musty smell," he said softly. He swallowed. "The nest. It's *here*."

Starting to panic, he knocked the heat duct and other debris off himself, scrambling to his feet. He used one hand to push himself to his feet, not seeing the queen racing towards him.

As one hairy spider leg touched his hand, Ross instinctively rolled out of the way, then jumped up, looking back at where the spider had been. She was gone. And he had no idea where.

There was a faint, skittering sound as the unseen spider made her way across the cellar floor from somewhere in the darkness. Terrified, Ross ran for the stairs, trying to open the door. It was locked.

"Help!" he shouted. "Someone help me!"

There was no answer.

"Collins!" he yelled, as loudly as he could. "I'm in here! *So's the nest!* And the queen is after me!"

There was still no answer. He was on his own.

The scratching sound of the queen's eight running legs was closer. Ross ran back down the steps, grabbing for the first weapon he could find — a shovel, leaning up against the cellar wall. Crouching in a low, defensive position, he slowly made his way around the cellar, searching for the queen.

He knocked over a wine rack — nothing. He brought a bicycle crashing to the floor — nothing. He swung the shovel across the potting table and swept it clean. Still, he found no spider.

But the spider was there, poised on a length of pipe, spinning its silken thread.

Hearing a little sound, Ross looked up, panicked by the thought that he might also be vulnerable to attack from above. The spider, however, swung out at him from *behind*. Ross whirled around, bringing his shovel up. The spider slammed against it and dropped to the floor. He thought.

Shaking, Ross, who was still holding onto the shovel, looked down to see where the spider might have fallen. As he scanned the dark floor, the spider crawled out of the crease in the shovel's blade and crept up the handle.

The spider started to step onto his hand, and Ross shouted, throwing the shovel away as hard as he could. It hit the electric panel — power for the entire house — and as the spider clung to the metal of the shovel, she was instantly electrocuted, turning into a bright spider X ray as she died.

"Therapy," Ross said weakly, and took a couple of deep breaths to try and calm down.

The nest. Now he had to find the nest.

"The thing we have to kill, the queen," he mumbled, looking around the floor for a flashlight, reciting the information that Collins had given him. "You'd see an egg sac — like your basic egg sac — about the size of a softball. . . ."

He found the flashlight in the pile of stuff he'd knocked off the potting table and picked it up, turning on the beam. He flashed it around the cellar. There, inside the annex, was the sac. Ross gasped, shocked by the size of it. The sac looked like no ordinary softball.

"Burn it," he said quietly, giving himself a little

pep talk. "I have to burn it." He glanced around, then saw his case of brandy. "Perfect," he said.

He picked up a bottle of his Napoleon brandy, then looked around for the furnace lighter. He flicked it on to test it, then broke the bottle open and carried it towards the annex.

Just as he was about to pour the brandy onto the egg sac, the male South American spider suddenly reared up from the wine rack to his left, mandibles twitching.

It was the biggest spider Ross had ever seen. It was his ultimate nightmare.

Chapter 23

Ross recoiled in fear and crashed into the wine rack to his right, bringing it down on himself. This set off a chain reaction, and other wine racks fell, one of the bottles shattering against his head. His head was badly gashed, and he blinked away the blood, staring at the spot where he'd seen the huge spider.

The spider was no longer there.

Ross looked around, then saw a large spider shadow against the wall — right above *his* shadow. The spider dropped down on Ross's head. Ross swept it off with his hand.

It landed on the floor, upside down, but quickly righted itself. Again, it charged. Ross, searching desperately for a weapon, found a case of brandy nearby. He grabbed one bottle and flung it at the spider.

The bottle smashed against the floor and the spider retreated. Then, Ross threw one bottle after another, aiming them like grenades. The creature dodged each of them, unscathed by the flying glass. It looked for the opportunity to attack again.

Ross had only one bottle left. He threw it, then looked around for another weapon. His eyes fell on a spray-paint canister. As he groped for it, the spider charged.

Ross grabbed the can with one hand, then fumbled for the furnace lighter with the other. He pressed down on the spray nozzle and flicked on the lighter — creating a spray-paint blowtorch.

The spider skidded to a halt, staring at the fire. Then it backed up a step or two.

"That's right," Ross said, and smiled a little, aiming the fire stream at him.

The spider continued to retreat.

Seizing the advantage, Ross began to extricate himself from the wine racks, keeping his eyes on the spider every second. But he needed both hands, and he had to stop spraying. Immediately, the spider came towards him again and, just as quickly, Ross started spraying fire again.

This time, the spider scurried underneath some debris and out of sight.

Ross struggled with the wine racks, finally managing to free himself. Then he sprayed some fire in the direction of the debris where the spider was hiding. It bolted out, heading for the wine racks on the opposite wall, Ross right behind it.

As he sprayed fire wildly, Ross began igniting small fires in the piles of debris in the cellar. The spider disappeared under the wine racks a fraction of a second ahead of the fire stream.

Ross stopped, looking at the first wine rack intently, seeing the spider's shadow on the wall behind it. He aimed a spray of fire at the shadow, but the spider had already moved out of the way, to the next wine rack.

Ross followed from wine rack to wine rack, shooting fire, the spider managing to escape each time. Now Ross couldn't find it at all and he scanned the room, his fear beginning to return.

He heard skittering along the pipes and looked up, trying to locate his enemy. He stopped again, now hearing an odd tinny sort of sound. Before Ross could figure out what it was, the spider came tearing out of the broken heating duct and leapt at him, landing on his shirt.

Ross dropped the furnace lighter and spray can, grabbed his shirt with both hands and tried to shake the huge spider off himself. He held the shirt away from his skin, trying to keep the spider's dripping fangs a safe distance away. He fell over the heating duct, knocking the spider off as he landed.

Ross lay in a pile of debris, eyes darting around the cellar, trying to find the spider. It had landed near the bottom of the stairs and was glaring right back at him. Paralyzed by arachnophobia, Ross tried to get up but found that he couldn't move. His breath came out in short bursts.

The spider came towards him, taking his time. Ross broke into a cold sweat, his eyes locked on the spider's eyes — all eight of them.

The spider stalked over, stopping a couple of inches away from Ross's foot. Slowly, very slowly, it reached out with one huge spider leg, touching Ross's foot. Then it crept up onto Ross's leg.

Ross stared, too terrified to move, almost hypnotized by fear, watching the spider.

"Ross!" Molly called, her voice coming faintly from somewhere outside. "Ross, where are you? Ross!"

The sound of his wife's voice startled Ross out of his arachnophobia, and he looked behind him as the spider climbed onto a board lying across Ross's stomach. Behind them, a pile of torched debris was now a raging inferno.

Ross slapped one end of the board on his stomach, catapulting the spider into the air. The spider landed in the fire and began writhing in the flames.

Ross dragged himself out of the way, watching the spider burn. Then he glanced up at the egg sac, his mouth falling open in horror.

It was beginning to hatch.

Ross grabbed a piece of wood and a rag, quickly making a homemade torch. Then he doused it with lighter fluid, getting ready to ignite the sac.

Suddenly, a spinning fireball raced towards him. Ross dropped the torch as he tried to duck out of the way.

It was a fight to the death, and the spider was refusing to die.

Chapter 24

Ross scrabbled like a crab, trying to stay out of the way of the furiously whirling fireball. He moved backwards, one hand falling onto the Ramset nail gun, his fingers closing around it.

The spider tore across a pool of brandy, leaving a trail of flames behind. Ross stared at this nightmare vision, raised the nail gun, and held it with both hands.

All ablaze, the spider lunged for him and Ross pulled the trigger of the nail gun. The nail pierced the spider and sent it hurtling backwards — right into the egg sac. The giant sac burst into flames and the spiders that were about to hatch were instantly destroyed.

The nail pinned the South American spider to the post, where it hung, fighting and wriggling in the flames. Then, finally, it died.

Ross let out his breath. "Thank God," he said.

"Don't mention it," said a cheerful voice above him. Then Delbert reached down through the smoke and flames and he and Molly pulled Ross out through the now-open cellar doors.

Completely exhausted, Ross toppled forward onto the lawn, trying to catch his breath.

It had been quite a night.

The lawn was crowded with firefighters, police officers, medics, and even a Ku-Band van from the local television station KNMA. Over by the barn, Atherton's body was being taken out on a gurney and placed inside a hearse.

Delbert stood in the driveway, tired but triumphant, surrounded by dead spiders and admiring Canaimans.

Ross, still somewhat dazed, stood a few yards away with Chris, surveying the spider corpses.

"Amazing," Ross said. "The big galoot killed all the spiders."

"Not all," Chris said.

Ross shot him a look.

"The ones he didn't nail are dead or dying," Chris said. "An abbreviated life cycle."

Ross sighed, relieved. "Like Atherton said."

Chris nodded. "But if you hadn't killed the queen . . ."

They both shuddered, not wanting to pursue the thought any further.

Mayor Bob came over, slinging an arm around Ross's shoulders as the television cameras moved in.

"Ross, let's assure the good citizens of Canaima

that this crisis is averted," he said, beaming into the cameras.

Ross shook his arm off. "Some other time," he said.

"Come on," the mayor said. "We're both 'people-people,' aren't we?"

Beyond them, Sheriff Parsons was giving one of the reporters an in-depth interview.

"After securing the scene at Jennings' barn," he said, "I quickly proceeded to outlying areas, where I visually verified that the arachnids were indeed expiring."

The mayor pushed him out of the way, getting in front of the cameras himself and pulling Ross over next to him.

"When Ross and I first liaised on this emergency," he said, "I thought to myself, The people have placed their trust in me. How can I best serve the people?"

Ross rolled his eyes and limped out of camera range, over to Molly and the kids, who were watching the fire unhappily.

"Hey," he said, "if it all goes up, how about something sort of — pre-postmodern?"

"How about moving back to San Francisco?" Molly said.

"*Moving?*" Ross said. "I like it here, Molly."

She stared at him. "But — everything you thought was true. All your worst fears were justified, we almost — "

"Shhh," Ross said suddenly.

She stopped talking, and they both listened.

"A cricket?" she said.

A small, cute cricket hopped across the grass.

Delbert hurried over, instantly ready with his insecticide.

"*Don't*," Ross said.

"Right," Delbert said, and wandered away.

Ross pulled his family close. He knew that, even though the house was burning, everything was going to be just fine.

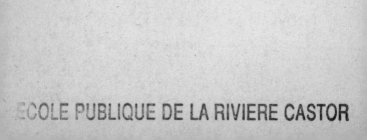
ÉCOLE PUBLIQUE DE LA RIVIERE CASTOR